C000297736

Investment in Love

Emily Walters

Investment in Love

Published by Emily Walters

Copyright © 2019 by Emily Walters

ISBN 978-1-07145-803-7

First printing, 2019

www.EmilyWaltersBooks.com

PRINTED IN THE UNITED STATES OF AMERICA

Dedication

I want to dedicate this book to my beloved husband, who makes every day in my life worthwhile. Thank you for believing in me when nobody else does, giving me encouragement when I need it the most, and loving me simply for being myself.

Table of Contents

CHAPTER 1 1

CHAPTER 2 10

CHAPTER 3 25

CHAPTER 4 36

CHAPTER 5 49

CHAPTER 6 56

CHAPTER 7 70

CHAPTER 8 87

CHAPTER 9 99

CHAPTER 10 111

CHAPTER 11 132

CHAPTER 12 149

EPILOGUE 155

WHAT TO READ NEXT? 158

ABOUT EMILY WALTERS 161

ONE LAST THING...162

Chapter 1

Calvin Barnard was at work at his job as a stockbroker when he got the call. He was sitting in front of his three computer monitors, watching the numbers on a share in an up-and-coming technology firm and getting just about ready to hit sell, when a phone rang.

He reached for the desk phone, blue eyes still on the monitor before him, but no noise came through the earpiece. *Oops.* That meant it was his personal cellphone. His strong hands fished around in a pocket to pull out the slim device. With the high-tech rectangle in his hand, he slid to accept the call, but his eyes never left the incoming data. *Was it time to sell?*

"Barnard," he said, pushing back one stray brown curl that insisted on falling over his ear despite his expensive haircut.

"Mr. Calvin Barnard?"

"Speaking."

"This is Walter Greenfeld, calling on behalf of the estate of Loretta Meyer." The voice on the other end of the phone was that of an older man, gravelly and dignified, and Calvin didn't recognize it at all.

"I'm sorry, say that again?"

"Mr. Barnard, my firm is settling the distribution of your Great-Aunt Loretta's estate. My name is Walter Greenfeld. I think it'd be best if we could talk in person."

Great-Aunt Loretta? Calvin finally looked away from the screens before him, reflexively pinching the bridge of his straight, Roman nose and sighing. He thought he remembered meeting a Great-Aunt Loretta once, way back before his mom had died. Curly white hair, thick glasses, but that was about all that came to mind. And now she was dead, apparently, if a lawyer wanted to talk about her estate.

The computer dinged with an update, and Calvin suddenly realized he'd been quiet for an awkwardly long time. "Look, Mr.—Mr. Greenfeld, you said? I'm just going to be honest with you: I only met my Great-Aunt Loretta once that I can recall. I'm sure she was a perfectly nice woman, and I wish I'd had a chance to get to know her, but as things stand, I don't know what her will and estate have to do with me."

"Mr. Barnard, I really think it would be best if we could talk in person. In matters like this I really prefer to meet face-to-face. I can fly to New York if necessary—I believe that's where you're located?"

"Uh, yeah, yeah I am." He shifted in his chair, rolling a pen between his fingers. "Can I ask where you're located if you'd need to fly to New York?" It hadn't even occurred to him that his great-aunt might have lived far away. But come to think of it, when he'd visited her with his mom, she had lived in Oregon somewhere.

"Greenfeld, Campton, and Associates is located in Portland, Oregon, but we have offices as far south as Carterville, which is where your great-aunt was living."

Calvin leaned back in his chair, propping his scuffed dress shoes on the desk before him. "Mr. Greenfeld, I appreciate your intentions with wanting to meet face-to-face, but I'm busy and it sounds like it would be a lot of trouble for you. I can't imagine that whatever Great-Aunt Loretta might have left me is worth all that time and effort to discuss. Could you make an exception and let me know on the phone?" *No way I'm flying to Oregon, and I doubt you actually want to come out here*, he thought to himself.

"Mr. Barnard, I'm actually certain it's worth the time."

"Well, what are we talking?"

Silence ticked by on the other end of the line before the lawyer finally spoke.

"Something in the realm of $10 million, Mr. Barnard, but there are some delicate conditions involved."

Calvin's feet fell off the desk and he dropped the pen.

"Ten million dollars?!"

***

Two days later, Calvin found himself leaving his tiny apartment for a meeting at a nearby café.

The place was incredibly nice, with towering ceilings and gently twinkling chandeliers. When he told the maître d' he was meeting Mr. Greenfeld, the man led him straight to a curtained-off alcove in the corner.

The elderly lawyer was tall and quite friendly looking—nothing like Calvin had been picturing on the phone. He shook hands with a firm but not too firm grip and settled in behind a sheaf of papers.

"I took the liberty of ordering us a pot of tea," the man said cheerfully, "but you won't hurt my feelings if you want to order something else."

"Tea is fine, thank you." Calvin actually wasn't that big on tea, but he'd rather get to the point quickly than wait around for a cup of strong coffee.

Mr. Greenfeld poured a steaming cup and slid it before the younger man.

Calvin stirred at it anxiously with a spoon. It didn't need stirring, but he didn't know how to open the conversation with this lawyer. He barely even remembered Great-Aunt Loretta. There had to be some mistake.

After the lawyer had precisely measured out two spoonfuls of sugar and stirred it into his tea, he took a slow sip. "I imagine you have a lot of questions."

Calvin laughed. "You could say that."

"You say you only met your great-aunt once?"

His dark blue eyes went solemn and he nodded. "I wish I'd gotten to know her, but the fact is I'd forgotten she existed until you called me."

The lawyer nodded slowly, creased face softening. "I never met her. One of our associates took her will. But it was well known that she was reclusive. She rarely left her house in Carterville, as far as I'm aware."

Calvin didn't even know what to say now, other than to yell "Tell me about the money!" but that was hardly polite. Unknowingly, he twisted up the cloth napkin between his fingers, catching the eye of the man across the table. Around them, the low murmur of diners and tinkling silverware drifted.

"I'm sorry, Mr. Barnard. I'm sure you're very anxious to hear the details of your great-aunt's estate. As I mentioned over the phone, we are talking a very large amount of money."

He moistened his dry throat before responding. "Ten million dollars." Surprisingly, Calvin's voice didn't shake, although he'd expected it to.

Mr. Greenfeld dabbed at his lips precisely. "Yes, $10 million. However, Loretta Meyer attached some very unusual, very specific provisions to the inheritance."

Calvin was pretty sure he didn't care what they were. He'd visit the woman's grave once a day or build a monument in her honor as big as the Statue of Liberty if that meant getting $10 million. "Go on," he said.

"Well, along with the liquidated wealth, which comes in the form of bonds, stock shares, and of course a lump sum in the bank, Loretta also willed you her home in Carterville, Oregon. It's an aging mansion—very beautiful, but in need of repair. The property is yours no matter what—"

After a long pause, Calvin nervously spoke. "But what?"

"But there are certain conditions on the monetary wealth. It's a very unusual requirement, Mr. Barnard, but allow me to reassure you in advance that it is legal."

The young stockbroker tilted his head, wondering just what Mr. Greenfeld was being so cryptic about.

Finally, the lawyer continued, looking uncomfortable. "According to your great-aunt's will, you are willed the entire remnant of her wealth. This inheritance is to be held provisional for a time of three months—beginning today, when I inform you of the condition—and if, at the end of that period, you have married a resident of Carterville, will be paid into your possession. If you fail to marry a Carterville woman by that date, the inheritance will be forfeit and shall instead be paid to a charity organization. Furthermore, your potential bride may not be paid for her part in the marriage, nor can she be informed of the conditions until after your wedding."

Calvin sat there stupidly for a long moment. So many questions raced through his mind that he didn't know where to start. *Marriage?* But he was only 25. He had been working so much there hadn't even been time to date. Sure, he wanted a wife and a family someday, but he also wanted to be a successful career man first. *And Carterville?* Where was that, even? He'd never heard of the town—and if it was in Oregon, that meant it was on the other side of the continent.

"Why me?" was the question that finally came out.

"I'm sorry?" Mr. Greenfeld looked puzzled, if decidedly more relaxed now that the news had been broken.

"Why did Aunt Loretta—Great-Aunt Loretta, I guess—leave everything to me? Why am I the one who has to—to—to marry? What about my cousins? Surely they have just as much or more connection to the woman as I did."

The lawyer shrugged, wrinkling up the shoulders of his crisp gray suit. "I'm sorry, Mr. Barnard, but I have no idea. All I know is that Ms. Meyer was of sound mind at the time she wrote this will, and that the conditions laid out within are legally binding."

"But *marriage?*"

Mr. Greenfeld shrugged again helplessly. "I know this must be overwhelming, but I'm telling you all I know. If you are willing to accept the conditions, you'll need to sign here, here, and here." He made a few X's on different sheets of paper. "Otherwise, let me know, and I will sign the funds over to the designated charity organization, and you will merely receive the deed to the house."

For one very long moment, Calvin sat frozen, staring at the papers. *Ten million dollars.* He couldn't even fathom the amount. Surely *anything* was worth $10 million, even a rushed marriage. He could just find some girl who appreciated money, marry her and divorce her quick as that, and then pay her generously for her troubles.

"Okay," he said, and reached for the pen.

Dozens of signed pages of legal papers, five hours of flight, four phone calls to his managers, three suitcases, and a 90-minute rental car drive later, Calvin found himself staring at a green sign nestled in among some evergreens.

"Welcome to Carterville, Oregon! Pop. 2,478."

Chapter 2

The GPS led him through a few small-town streets and back into open forest. *That's it? I thought the house was in Carterville,* Calvin thought. In truth, the address was technically within the boundaries of the town, but the small dirt road that led to it was a few more turns up the highway.

Dim memories flashed through his mind as he drove. He and his mom had visited Carterville once when he was in middle school, but nothing seemed familiar. He remembered a long drive and the forest—and an argument between his mom and her Aunt Loretta, but that was it.

He tapped his fingers nervously as he rattled up the rough dirt road. It seemed far too bumpy to lead to a house, but the GPS said he was on the right track. Calvin had high hopes—Mr. Greenfeld referred to it as a mansion, after all. Finally, he came around a last corner and the GPS beeped. "You have arrived at your destination!"

Calvin stared in disappointment when he unlocked the creaky door. The outside was nice enough— colonial style in cream and brown—but the inside was mostly very dusty. He peered in room after room, looking at flowery décor and faded drapes, and finally just collapsed on the soft bed in what seemed to be a guest room as jet lag caught up.

At first, his intention was just to relax and regroup before taking an inventory. Mr. Greenfeld had made it quite clear that the mansion—and everything in it— was his to sell and was outside of the will provisions. That meant it was Calvin's backup plan if the whole wedding scheme fell through. He could get a couple hundred thousand out of the place, probably—no small sum—and if he sold the curios and other items inside, that amount would be increased. But cleaning was going to be hard work, and he was *so* tired... so Calvin let his eyes drift shut.

The next morning, a strange noise tickled at Calvin's ears until his bleary eyes forced themselves open. For one blank moment, he had absolutely no idea where he was. The walls were decorated with dusty paintings of flowers, and he was pretty sure he was sleeping in shoes and a belt, not to mention slacks and a button-down shirt. Feeling stiff, he pushed up on his elbows and looked toward the end of the bed. Yup. He was still wearing everything from yesterday. God, it was *bright* in the unknown room. He squinted out a gap in the rose-colored curtains at the tops of trees before recognition hit.

He was at his Great-Aunt Loretta's house. His dead Great-Aunt Loretta, who he'd only met once, who had left him $10 million if he married someone from this tiny town.

The strange high-pitched noise that had woken him up was definitely birdsong. Still groggy, Calvin shoved two hands through his mussed hair and stretched his back. As soon as he was fully awake, he was eager to get to work. There were only three months (less, actually, since his vacation time wasn't going to stretch the full three months) to fix up this house, get it sold, and find a wife. A *wife*, of all things.

Calvin decided to focus on the house first. It was much less terrifying than the thought of finding a wife. He jogged downstairs and grabbed a phone book. He flipped through, skimming headings until one caught his eye: "Interior Decorators and Designers." Perfect! His heart sank when he saw that there was only one small ad under that category, but still, this could be a solution to the house problems.

"Parker Home Design," it said in flowery script. "Interior Design Consultation! Furnishings and Decor! Upholstery and Flooring! Home Appliances! Affordable Prices!"

Calvin noted the address and rushed to get dressed. Surely someone there would be able to fix up the house for him! Market value on this had to be a couple hundred thousand at the least, so even if the service was on the pricy side, he was sure to make a profit.

After quickly brushing his teeth, dressing, and splashing some water on face and hair, he fled the house, grateful to be free of the dusty air, and bounced back down the road into tiny Carterville.

In the morning light, the sky was a beautiful shade of pure blue and the forest was a velvety green in the crisp, fresh air. The landscape was beautiful, but the town felt very empty after being walled in by skyscrapers. Carterville had been empty when he'd driven through the day before, and it wasn't any busier today. The place was barely big enough to be called a town, with only a few streets and three two-story buildings, one of which was the old-fashioned courthouse. Thankfully, a familiar fast food chain's golden arches had made it even out to Carterville, so Calvin was able to get his morning coffee from a chirpy teenage employee.

Finally, the sun had risen high enough that the interior design place would probably be open. Calvin typed the address into the on-car GPS and hit the road again.

***

Elizabeth Parker whistled quietly as she stacked bottles of carpet cleaner onto the metal shelf—or rather, she tried to whistle. She'd never quite mastered the skill, though, and instead a shrill, breathy sound was all that came from her lips. The bells on the front door jingled, and a moment later, the bell at the register dinged. She called, "Be right up!" without looking away from her armload of products. With the last one stacked neatly on the shelf, she finally spun and stepped quickly toward the front.

"What can I do for you?" she asked cheerily, welcoming smile turning to a confused expression when she saw the customer who stood before her. He wore fancy-looking pressed khakis and a blue dress shirt. She wondered why he was dressed up. She also wondered who he was and why he was so absurdly handsome—a pair of dark blue eyes gleamed at her when their gazes met, and she had a stupid urge to run her hands through his curly brown hair.

"Hi," she said a little breathlessly. Then, "What can I do for you?"

"I'm looking for a full floor-to-ceiling renovation." He said it brusquely, without even bothering to return her greeting, and Ellie felt the beginnings of irritation.

"I'm sorry?"

"A full renovation. Furniture, carpet, appliances, paint—everything."

"For *what?*" She hadn't meant to sound quite so confused, but this man clearly wasn't a local, and she couldn't think of anyone who needed a full remodel.

The man's navy blue eyes went from looking distant to looking irritated. "A *house.*" His voice had the edge of a regional accent that she couldn't quite place.

14

She flushed. "I gathered that, yes. I was wondering which house."

"Oh." Silence reigned for a moment before he opened his full lips again. "Uh, up on the hill. My Great-Aunt Loretta's old place. Big purple house."

"You're remodeling Miss Meyer's old place?" For a moment, Ellie was excited, but then she remembered the resources at her disposal. She bit her lip anxiously, glancing around the small, familiar store. "Um, I'll do whatever I can to help, but I have to be really honest with you: We've never done a full renovation before."

Her mind was racing. It had seemed so exciting back in college, when the design degree was almost in her grasp and she had sweet-talked her dad into adding those services to their ad. Sure, she technically knew how to do it—in fact, Ellie had been hoping for years that someone would give her free reign with the design and furnishing of their house. She had years of experience with appliance and furniture sales, as well as carpet installation and that sort of thing (from working with her dad), plus a keen eye for design (honed by her college work). It was just that so far, she hadn't actually had any big clients, and now that Dad was gone, the task seemed suddenly intimidating.

Calvin eyed the pretty girl before him in irritated surprise. Sure, the town had looked even tinier today than on the way through yesterday, and this home improvement store had seemed small. But he had just assumed that they had a big warehouse somewhere.

This shop girl was pretty enough—golden brown waves gathered up in a messy bun, big brown eyes, and a waist so tiny he thought he could close his hands around it. Unfortunately, he was pretty sure she was also dumb. At least, she was looking at him like she could barely comprehend what he was saying.

"You've got to be kidding. I checked the phone book. You're the only place under interior design."

She shifted before him, looking uncomfortable. "We do interior design and renovation! It's just that we've never had anyone request such an extensive renovation before." Ellie bit back the sassier remarks that wanted to come flying out of her mouth. Who did this guy think he was? Just because he was rich didn't mean he was smarter than her. She wouldn't have listed the services if she wasn't qualified to provide them.

The man spoke again, looking irritated. "Can I speak to—" he turned to look back at the door "—Parker?"

Parker Home Design. Ellie recited the name, feeling a twinge of pain at the thought of her dad proudly hanging the sign twenty years ago. "That would be me. Elizabeth Parker. Everyone calls me Ellie," she said, letting a slight edge creep into her tone.

She held out her hand, and at last the handsome-but-rude man seemed to remember his manners. "Calvin," he said, shaking her hand with a firm, dry grip. She forgot her irritation in the frisson that sparked in her hand at the man's touch.

As he gripped her delicate hand, Calvin found his eyes drawn back across Ellie's heart-shaped face and full lips to the purple T-shirt and jeans that she wore. They clung to petite curves, and he wondered again about the question of marrying a Carterville girl. *It really didn't matter if she was smart—just if he could stomach a three-month relationship with her.* He thought spending three months with this girl might be an easy task, as long as she let him look at her beautiful self.

On second thought, she had narrowed her eyes into a suspicious, unfriendly glare. Maybe this Ellie wasn't such a likely prospect. "Look," he said, "could you at least give it a look, give me an estimate, that kind of thing? I can't afford to have furniture trucked out from Portland. You're really my only option, if your business actually does home renovation and interior design."

Ellie wondered how he could afford a full renovation if he was so tight on money, but if he was going to pay her, who was she to question it? Of course, if he kept eyeing her like she was a piece of meat, maybe she wouldn't accept his money after all. It was flattering to have a handsome, sophisticated rich boy looking at her like that, but she wasn't going to be swayed by a handsome face.

She broke off her train of thought, suddenly remembering that he—Calvin, apparently—needed a response. "Um, sure," she said quickly, feeling a blush spread across her cheeks. Nope, she couldn't turn down his money. The man was wearing expensive leather oxfords, hinting that he had plenty of money to spend. *And he looks good wearing them, too,* said her mind before she could shush it. "Why don't we sit down and talk about everything that you think you'll need?"

"Sure," said Calvin. "Is there any chance we could do that over lunch right now? The sooner you and your team can start, the better." He followed the statement with a quick half smile that made his eyes crinkle up adorably.

Ellie agreed, and said that she would drive her own car to the restaurant and he could follow her in his vehicle.

She led the way to a small restaurant labelled Susie's Sandwiches in a small green SUV, with Calvin driving the rental car behind her. They pulled in and parked in a small paved lot, populated by only by a few other cars, and Calvin mused over the easy parking. The free, empty public lot was in such contrast to the competitive parking he had experienced last time he went out in New York.

Speaking of… "So, um, Ellie," he started awkwardly, staring at her slim form from the back as she hopped out of the car and headed toward the restaurant, "is there much of a nightlife around here?" He needed to figure out where the suitable place to meet women was.

"Nightlife?" The pretty shop girl turned and looked genuinely confused.

"You know, like a singles scene?"

She started laughing and he felt his cheeks redden slightly. "Singles scene? In Carterville? Well, there's a dance at the community center once a month—this month's is tomorrow, actually—and we have a decent Italian café that lights up pretty at night."

Calvin's heart sank. How was he going to meet a woman, much less win her heart, if that was all that was available to him? He couldn't exactly lay on the charm and sophistication at a community center dance. The laughter in Ellie Parker's eyes stung, and he quickly changed the subject. "Listen, did you know my great-aunt at all?"

As they seated themselves in a booth, she said, "I didn't really know Miss Meyer, sorry. She didn't come out much. She'd worked out a delivery system with most businesses around town."

Calvin mulled this over, biting at the inside of his cheek thoughtfully. "So she just stayed up here all alone?"

Ellie nodded, looking momentarily saddened. She tucked a loose strand of hair behind her ear and said, "Yeah. I'm sorry."

It *was* sad, now that he thought about it. Why had his great-aunt been all alone? She'd never tried to reach out to the family, and the requisite Christmas cards had gone unanswered. When his mom had been alive, she'd sent a card to every family member—including Great-Aunt Loretta—every holiday season. Most had responded, but Great-Aunt Loretta had stayed silent and distant. And now here he was, with a will that entitled him to a pile of money, and a hundred puzzling questions.

"It's okay," he said quickly. She couldn't ask too many questions or he might slip up and let on about the strange inheritance situation.

His train of thought was interrupted by the middle-aged waitress who came to take their order, and by the time she left he remembered that he was trying to get a wife. *Time to put on the charm.*

"So," he said, "let's talk about whatever kind of magic you're going to work on the house."

Ellie was a little suspicious of the sudden easy humor in his voice, but at the same time she couldn't help blushing from the comment. "Well, I guess it depends what you want. We should talk about what kind of style you're looking to bring to the place, types of furnishings, that sort of thing. Then I can give you a sort of preliminary guesstimate of price range and how long it might take, but we'll need to actually walk through the space before I can give you solid numbers."

Calvin shrugged helplessly, looking dramatically bewildered. "My apartment came pre-furnished! I've never thought about this in my life!"

Ellie found herself laughing, almost against her will. "Sorry, I suppose it must be overwhelming." He grinned boyishly at her in response, and her heart warmed into curiosity. "Apartment where?"

"New York."

"Like New York, New York?"

"Oh yes. High-rises. Steel and glass. Modern, sleek, beautiful—none of this old dusty stuff." He gestured around, pointing either at the décor of Susie's or the town in general. "Uh, not that this doesn't have its charm."

Well, that certainly put an end to his attractiveness. Ellie absolutely hated it when city folk were close-minded about the appeals of a small town—and Carterville was a nice place to be. She didn't want to work with a man who couldn't see that. Too bad the store desperately needed the business.

Say something, Calvin, darn it, he told himself firmly. "Quaint little place like this would be a novelty in Manhattan," he said aloud. Surely this was the way to charm Ellie Parker. She'd looked adorably surprised when he'd said he was from New York. A sweet girl from a small town like this would be dazzled by the big city he was used to.

Across the table, Ellie gritted her teeth to keep her eyes from rolling. "I'm sure," she said politely. Who did this Calvin Barnard think he was? Sure, Carterville was different from a big city, but some people actually preferred things that way. She'd never had any interest in busy streets, hours of infuriating traffic, and giant, imposing skyscrapers.

Without much of a response, Calvin kept talking anxiously. "When do things close around here? 8 p.m. or so? Strange to see it so dark last night. The city just glows at night out my window."

Ellie took a slow, steadying breath. This man was pushing all her buttons in the exact wrong way. One more braggy comment about the big city and the novelty of an unfamiliar handsome face was going to wear off.

Maybe he could feel the force of her irritation, because she watched him nervously start twirling a fork again. Ellie tried to be polite and reply to his comment. "Yes, 8 if you're lucky. A lot of places close around 5. It was definitely an adjustment when I moved home after college. Corvallis—where I went to school—isn't a big city by any means, but it certainly is bigger and better lit than Carterville."

Calvin was too startled to be tactful. "*You* went to college?" As soon as the words crossed his lips, he knew his mistake, but it was too late to rephrase.

Ellie's eyes narrowed and the nostrils of her button nose flared. "Yes? Is that a surprise to you?"

He reached frantically for a way to fix his blunder. "Um, sorry, I didn't mean—it's just—backwoods towns are usually less educated, and I figured this place didn't seem too big on modern life…"

"What, so we're all a bunch of uneducated hicks?" Ellie jumped up angrily, BLT forgotten. "Let me tell you something, Mr. Barnard. We may be a bunch of hicks out here in Carterville, but we *chose* to stay here. We have college degrees and job skills and intelligent thoughts—and we have a heck of a lot better manners than city people like you. I'll give you a piece of advice. Fix up your great-aunt's house, and then sell it to someone who will appreciate it and get out of Carterville. We don't need your rude attitude and snobby judgment." Feeling self-righteous, she threw down her napkin and flounced out the door.

Calvin sat frozen for a moment, totally stunned. *Well, so much for choosing Ellie Parker as his Carterville bride.* The waitress came and dropped—literally dropped—his sandwich plate with a glare. *Great. It looked like Ellie wasn't the only Carterville resident he had alienated.* He sighed and buried his face in his hands. The plan was off to a bad start.

Chapter 3

Ellie fumed the whole way back to the shop, jerking angrily at the steering wheel of her little SUV. Thank God she'd driven herself instead of riding down in Calvin's shiny little rental car. It looked expensive, just like everything else he had, though she supposed it might just be a New York thing. *Her car was sensible.* It might not be glossy or especially pretty, but it had four-wheel drive and could handle a snowstorm.

She pulled into the parking lot of the shop and yanked her keys out of the ignition with a cheerful-sounding jingle that ill-befitted her mood. *God, what an infuriating man!* The small brunette itched to give him a piece of her mind.

Little did she know, only a few blocks away, Calvin was thinking the same thing. His guilt had lasted through about half his sandwich—which was delicious—and then he started to rethink things. Who was Ellie Parker to go making assumptions about what he was trying to say?

He grimaced when he remembered his words, biting at his cheek. It had come out all wrong. He hadn't been trying to say that Ellie Parker was stupid—it was clear now that she was pretty sharp, actually. It was just surprising that someone in a tiny town like this would have a college degree. *How is that insulting, anyway? You don't need a college degree to be smart.* Calvin's dad hadn't had a degree, but he was brilliant. It was pretty clear that the beautiful Miss Parker was one of those small-town residents who was absolutely determined to hate city people.

But okay, even if the way he'd said it might have sounded bad, there was no need to yell and stomp off. She hadn't even given him a chance to explain himself. Those shiny brown eyes and that curvy little body were not enough to make up for a nasty temper. Calvin crossed her off the imaginary list in his head. Problem was, she was the only girl on that list so far. There would be more options, surely—he just had to find them.

He finished the last crumbs of his roast beef sandwich, which was delicious, and stood to leave. At the last moment, he remembered to drop a large tip on the table. Maybe it would save his reputation, even if he'd managed to irritate the waitress with his earlier words to Ellie.

Calvin didn't really want to head back up to the purple monstrosity, but it wasn't like there was anything to do in town. He thought vaguely of trying to hang around somewhere to meet women, but he only had to drive a block to realize that this was an unlikely plan. There was simply nowhere to go. Tiny public library: possible, but unlikely. Couple of cafés and restaurants, but not too many of those and he'd just eaten. One pub, but drinking at noon wasn't going to win anyone over. Tiny public park full of kids would look creepy.

Right. Purple monstrosity it was.

The road lurched the car around absurdly as usual. *God, was it too much to ask for pavement?* He'd have to have it paved before putting it on the market. No buyer was going to suffer through three miles of bouncing and still be cheerful at the end. He firmed up his square jaw as the car juddered along, trying to focus on selling the house and getting $10 million. When he finally arrived and tossed open the old squeaky door, he remembered what a mess his great-aunt's house was. There was a very good chance he'd have to apologize enough that Ellie would still take on the job. He didn't know how else to deal with the faded drapes and crumbling carpets. This was his guaranteed income, but right now there was no way it would even get market value.

Hmm… Calvin just stood there, watching the sunlight filter through the dust motes and feeling helpless. This was so clearly another person's private space. It felt incredibly invasive to him to start digging through cabinets and throwing things out. Rationally, he knew that his great-aunt was dead and gone, but it was hard to remember that standing there in a house that looked like she might walk in at any minute.

He found himself wandering room to room, trying to find a suitable place to start. It was a big house. Downstairs, there was the outdated kitchen, in colors straight from the 1970s; a beautiful wood-paneled dusty dining room; *two* living rooms, one with a fireplace done up in dark wood and pink furniture, and one covered in a nasty puke-green color, and a bathroom—also pink.

And *everything* was flower-print. Calvin would have hated it on principle, but a tiny part of him was just happy to glean any understanding of his Great-Aunt Loretta. He was suddenly hungry to know her, now that it was too late. Why had she even had millions of dollars? Their family wasn't rich. He shuffled lightly through the papers on the tabletop, hoping for clues. Under a light layer of fluffy dust, there were a few bills, bank statements, stock investment reports, that sort of thing. Calvin skimmed them briefly and whistled in appreciation at the stocks she'd held. All of them were very good investments.

Feeling resolute about cleaning, he headed upstairs and tugged open one of the doors to reveal something similar to a library. A few shelves were entirely full of books, but many were also decorated with various curios. Most were shiny, and yes, many were pink or purple. A bouquet of old, dried-up flowers stood in a vase on the central table. It was dusty, and Calvin found himself wondering if someone had sent his Great-Aunt Loretta flowers.

Had she had a beau at some point? The answer was likely to be yes, based on sheer probability.

Grandma Maude would have known. Loretta was her sister, after all. For a moment, Calvin was lost in memories of his plump, sweet old grandma. She'd been gone for twelve years now, since even before his mom had died, but he still got a little wistful at the memory of one of her big, tight hugs. For the first time, staring around at this dust-filled house, he was struck with the realization of all the things he'd never asked his grandmother—or his mother, for that matter.

For the first time in too long, Calvin pulled his cell out of his pocket and dialed his dad's number.

He got the voicemail and left a quick message. "Hey Dad, it's me. I was just wondering if you had my Aunt Sheila's phone number—my mom's sister? You can just text it to me if you're busy. Thanks."

***

Back at Parker Home Design, Ellie wasn't feeling productive at all. There were very few customers, but she had plenty to do in the back office. She kept trying to sit down and work at the computer, too— but her mind wasn't on budget-balancing.

Instead, she kept thinking of a curly-headed New Yorker and his stuck-up attitude. Why did Calvin Barnard have to be so handsome? If he was ugly or

29

old it would have been so much easier to dismiss him. And the man didn't have that overly polished look that businessmen often got. He looked rugged enough to climb a mountain, with that strong jaw and Roman nose, softened just barely by the blue eyes and curly brown hair. But the personality… that was another matter. Why were charming, attractive men always such cads?

Oh well. It didn't matter. Except apparently it *did*, since she kept picturing that one honest smile she'd gotten out of the guy before he started being an ass.

She kicked a gray filing cabinet drawer shut and glared at the paperwork. The worst part was that now—after she'd stomped off like a princess—she was remembering why she'd agreed to do the remodel in the first place. The shop wasn't exactly operating at a profit this year. Maybe Dad had possessed a knack for selling home renovation items that she lacked—or maybe it was just the economy. There were only so many families in Carterville, after all, and it wasn't like they all needed the kitchen remodeled every year.

And, of course, the Internet reached even her tiny hometown. They couldn't stock too many options here in the small storefront, and more often than not, when Ellie said, "I can order it in for you in that color," the customers got impatient and just ordered it online themselves.

Ellie sighed wistfully, shoving her wavy hair up into a messy bun, and let herself dream of the store she'd planned when she was still in college, before her dad had died. She'd had big dreams back then—an expanded storefront with a warehouse out back, room-style displays that showed off her interior design abilities, the whole shebang. But then Dad had gotten sick and the medical bills for his chemotherapy treatment had taken everything they had, and once he was gone, Mom had been too broken up to even think about this store.

Pushing the chair back from the desk, Ellie got up and walked out into the fluorescent-lit storefront. She loved this place, really—it was in her blood. But an upgrade sure would be nice.

What she really ought to do was call Calvin Barnard and apologize. *Crap.* She hadn't gotten his phone number. Well, she'd give it a day or two so her bruised pride could adapt to the idea, and then drive up to the purple mansion and apologize in person. Her teeth were already gritting at the thought though. *He* was the one who should have been saying sorry— but she sure needed the business.

And it wouldn't exactly hurt to see that handsome face again. He probably wasn't even as cute as she remembered. *Blue eyes, strong jaw, so what?* She had a date tomorrow, too—a date she'd almost forgotten, but nonetheless. She didn't need any attention from Calvin Barnard with his khakis and his fancy oxfords.

Letting Bill Carlisle take her to the monthly community center dance tomorrow wasn't something to get excited about, exactly, but it was an excuse to dress up pretty and forget her cares for a few hours. Sure, at the end of the night she'd have to fend off Bill and explain to him for the fifteenth time that she'd agreed to go as a friend only, but the dancing could be fun. For once, the small-town gossip around the punch bowl might be enjoyable too, since it would be directed at the "uppity-New-York-city-boy" instead of Ellie herself.

She laughed quietly to herself, thinking of how the townspeople would lance the arrogant man, and then closed up the shop and drove home to pick out an outfit. It was almost five o'clock anyway, and something in Calvin Barnard's dismissive attitude had her wanting to look her best. He probably wouldn't be at the dance, but still. For some reason, she wanted to really get dolled up, like she hadn't in years.

Without bothering to be neat, Ellie tossed purse and keys on the granite kitchen counter and went straight to the bedroom closet. The dance wasn't until the next evening, but she wanted to have time to shop if her old clothes weren't suitable anymore.

Her hands reached first for one of the casual cotton dresses she usually wore, but no, that was too simple.

Instead, she flipped through to the back of the closet—things she hadn't worn since college. *There it is.* Silky black fabric slid under her fingers as she pulled out her old, favorite little black dress. It was an A-line cut with a flared skirt that she knew flared prettily during dancing, and a deep V-neck in the front. *This* would teach Calvin Barnard not to write off small-town girls.

After a moment, she realized her thoughts and blushed, shoving the dress back in the front of the closet.

"No more thinking about him, Ellie," she said aloud. "He's not going to be there, even if you're hoping you can show off for him."

***

Calvin had been wandering around the house for hours. He'd finally decided to take an inventory of the items to see if anything could be sold, but it was taking a lot longer than expected. Three pages of the pad were filled front and back, and he hadn't even gone near the books or other small items.

He was exhausted.

When he started to get hungry again and realized he still hadn't managed to get any groceries, the thought of a simple cost-benefit analysis suddenly occurred to him. Time to get house on the market: potentially forever, if today's time investment was any indication.

Okay, not quite forever. But realistically, this was going to take hours of hard work nearly every day for weeks, with a payoff of say $500,000. Finding a wife (as ludicrous as it sounded): lots of time, but easy, enjoyable work. Payoff: $10 million.

The answer was obvious. Sure, the house needed to go on the market, but that could happen at any time. Worst case he sat on it for a year and came back to finalize the sale next vacation. But the inheritance was going to expire in three months if he couldn't find a Carterville woman to marry. It made more sense to find himself a girl to start dating—one who seemed like she would be amenable to marriage. One who *wasn't* Ellie Parker.

But just then his phone buzzed. "New Message from Dad." For a moment, Calvin couldn't remember why his father would be texting him, but then his earlier questions came to mind.

"I only have an old phone number," the message said, and then listed a number.

Without pausing to think about it, Calvin tapped the screen and called the number. He was second-guessing himself by the third ring, but right then a female voice picked up and for a split second it sounded like his mother. The similarity froze him, and the woman spoke again.

"Hello? Anyone there?"

Calvin found his voice. "Is this Sheila?"

"It is."

"Hi, Aunt Sheila," he said with a dry throat. "It's Calvin. Ann's son. I have some questions about Grandma and Aunt Loretta."

Chapter 4

An almost unbearable silence stretched out on the other end, and when his aunt finally spoke again she sounded choked with emotion.

"Calvin? Is that really you?"

"It is," he said, trying to sound cheerful.

"Oh, Calvin, honey, we haven't heard from you since... well, since Ann's funeral."

His eyes prickled at the memory of that painful day, and he cleared his throat gruffly. "I'm sorry," he said suddenly. He was sorry, too. Why had he never tried to contact his mother's sister?

"Oh, honey," she said softly. "It's okay. We love you just the same."

Another silence emerged, but this one felt more peaceful. When Calvin was about to speak, his aunt beat him to it. "You said you had questions about Mom and Aunt Loretta?"

"Um, yes. I realized I don't know anything about how they grew up or anything like that. I never had a chance to talk to Grandma about it."

"Oh, sure," Aunt Sheila said kindly. "Well, let's see, where shall I start? Can you talk for a while?"

"Oh yes," said Calvin. "Take as long as you need."

"Well, hmm. Mom was born in the early 1930s, and Loretta was a little bit younger. They grew up in some tiny little mountain town in Oregon."

"Carterville?" Calvin asked eagerly.

"Yes, that sounds right," she answered. He peered around the house with new eyes, wondering if this was where his grandmother had been raised. It looked too new, though.

"Mom always said she grew up in a tiny little shack," his aunt continued. *Well, that answered that question.* "I think their daddy was a miner or logger, something like that—and they were poor, real poor. Their mom died when they were just little kids. I'm not sure how. I don't know if Mom even knew, but if she did she never said."

Calvin made a sympathetic, interested noise, eager to unravel the mystery. If they'd started poor, how had Great-Aunt Loretta gotten $10 million?

"Now, what your Grandma Maude told me the few times I got her to open up about it, was that her dad went downhill fast. She said he took to drinking. I've always wondered if he was abusive, but no one ever said." Aunt Sheila's voice softened at the memory, and she paused briefly before continuing. "I think Mom pretty much ended up raising Aunt Loretta, though. And I know she did really well in school, and that's how she ended up getting the teaching position in California, because someone recommended her. Then she met my dad—your Grandpa John—and got married when she was just 19. The rest, as they say, is history."

"Wow," said Calvin, unsure of how else to respond. This was a big spread of new information—but unfortunately it didn't answer most of his questions. He decided to proceed carefully, since he didn't want to tell Aunt Sheila about the inheritance. He was afraid he'd hurt her feelings. After all, surely she ought to have had some claim on her aunt's riches. "Um, what about Great-Aunt Loretta?" he asked, trying to sound casual.

Aunt Sheila inhaled sharply. "Oh, Calvin, honey, I don't know if anyone told you, but Aunt Loretta, she passed…"

Calvin fought the urge to smack himself in the forehead. "Sorry, Aunt Sheila! I should have been more clear. I know that she passed on recently. I was just hoping to learn more about her and Grandma's lives."

"Oh, okay," the older woman said. "Well, let's see. I think she moved out to California a little while after Mom and Dad did, but she didn't stay too long before heading back to Oregon. Mom never said much. I think she was pretty withdrawn her whole life. I know she was never much interested in visits from me and the kids. She visited a couple times when your mom and I were growing up, and we used to write letters, but eventually she just kinda fell off the map. Last time we talked was not too long after your mom died, I think."

"Hmm," said Calvin. "Did she ever get married or anything like that?"

"Nope," said his aunt. "She was pretty much a recluse, so far as I know. Maybe a few suitors back when they were young—her and your grandma were apparently quite the beauties back in their day." He could hear the smile in her voice.

Calvin chuckled at the information, but his mind was racing trying to put it all together in terms of the inheritance and the house. If Great-Aunt Loretta had been a poor recluse, where had the money come from? Had she been robbing banks or something? If so, was the money legal now?

This bit of fancy was banished when Aunt Sheila spoke again. "So Calvin, honey, tell me about you. You sound all grown up." She sounded wistful, and Calvin put his full attention on the phone conversation.

"I don't know if I'd say all grown up," he responded with a smile.

"What about a job? You must be working by now."

"Sure," he said. "I have a position as a stockbroker with Lincoln & Bosch in New York, actually."

"Oh wow," Aunt Sheila said. "You really are grown up. What about a girl? Married?"

Calvin nearly twitched at the question. What was he supposed to say? *No girlfriend at the moment, but I expect to be married within the next three months.* Instead, he said, "Nothing too serious," and left it vague.

"Well, I'm sure you'll find someone," she said sweetly.

I sure hope so. And fast, he thought. Suddenly, he added aloud, "When there is someone serious, Aunt Sheila, maybe you could meet her. Maybe I could come visit sometime."

"That would be lovely," she said, voice soft with emotion.

They tied the call up after a few more minutes of small talk, and Calvin sat rubbing his tired ear and thinking. Great-Aunt Loretta's inheritance was more of a mystery than ever—and his aunt had reminded him that he needed some prospects fast if he was going to be married in three months.

What had Ellie said? The pretty brunette had mentioned something when he'd asked about the singles scene—a community dance. His brain immediately provided pictures of something out of the movie *Grease,* but he quickly banished the visions of poodle skirts. Just because this was a small town didn't mean they were stuck in the past.

The next thing Calvin envisioned was a nightclub, but that didn't seem right either. No, if anything, this would be like a middle school dance. Paper streamers, weak punch, bad music…

And women. Lots of young, single women, hopefully.

With a plan firmly in mind, Calvin felt more confident. Organization always helped him, so he sat down with a pen and paper and titled a list "To-Do."

- o Groceries
- o Look for consignment stores
- o Apologize to Ellie Parker?
- o Or find home design alternative…
- o Get details on comm. dance
  - Need ticket?
  - Bring anything?
  - Dress code

Dress code wouldn't really be a problem—he'd brought a pretty wide selection of clothing in his suitcases. But he did want to make sure he didn't look awkward, or offend anyone.

The day went by quickly. It turned out there were no grocery delivery services in Carterville—not that he was really surprised—so Calvin drove back into town to do his shopping. While he was there, he was able to not only get ingredients for a week's worth of meals, but also to stop and talk to the owner of a dusty little store called Treasures 'n' Things that looked like it might sell some of his aunt's old things for him.

Kathy of Treasures had been positively ecstatic at the possibility of going through "old Miss Loretta's" decorative belongings, and she'd offered to come up within the next week and make an offer on anything she wanted. That made things pretty simple for Calvin, and he resolved to have a complete list of items ready for review as soon as possible. Conveniently, she'd also had a stack of flyers for the community dance, so Calvin had grabbed one to take home with him and then headed back up the hill to the house.

The flyer said "All Welcome!" and advertised dancing, a raffle, and food. Calvin decided to play it safe with another casual outfit of khakis and a button-up shirt. He'd noticed that the residents of Carterville seemed to wear jeans and T-shirts most of the time, and he didn't want to look like a fish out of water by wearing too nice of an outfit.

After making himself a simple omelet for dinner, he pulled his to-do list back across the table in front of him. The pen made quick strokes through "groceries," "consignment store," and "community dance," and then he was just left with one item.

Calvin stared at the words for a while. He couldn't explain why he hadn't just called her and apologized. He told himself that he didn't want to work with her anymore—but he hadn't looked for another business to replace Parker Home Design either. *The practical solution would be to call her right now...* But instead he stood up and headed back to the library to inventory Great-Aunt Loretta's belongings.

***

Ellie cheerfully hummed her way through the next day's work, anticipation building for the dance. She couldn't explain why she was so excited to go to the community dance this time, since Bill wasn't too exciting and she'd been many, many times before, but a current of energy ran through her every time she thought about it.

Maybe it was having the chance to really dress up. She usually stuck to practical clothes like jeans and a T-shirt.

She pulled out all the stops—eyeliner, shimmery nude eye shadow that made her brown eyes glitter, pretty peach lipstick, curled hair, and a pushup bra. Top it all off with her favorite black dress and a pair of black velvet heels, and she was—*Well, not too bad. Not bad at all, actually*, she thought as she looked in the mirror. There was time for just one spritz of her favorite floral perfume and then a knock sounded on the door.

"Come on in," she called from her bedroom, transferring things from her purse to a smaller clutch.

"Hi, Ellie," said Bill Carlisle's familiar voice. She could hear him closing the door and shuffling around in the living room.

"I'm all ready to go if you are," she said, still fidgeting with her purse as she walked down the hall.

He didn't say anything. She looked up, blinking in confusion, and tried to figure out why Bill was just standing there quiet. The stocky man stood there gaping at her in the light from the lamp, lips slightly parted.

"Holy shi—Excuse me," he said all in a rush, clearing his throat gruffly. "Wow, Ellie. You look... *gorgeous.*"

She felt herself flush pink at the man's reaction. "Don't be silly," she said automatically. "I just felt like dressing up. Haven't in a while."

Bill was still standing there, baseball cap in hand. Ellie rolled her eyes. "You all ready?"

"Uh, yeah. Yeah, sorry," he said. "Truck's running outside."

The sun was just setting as they drove toward the community center, and Ellie noticed self-consciously that Bill kept glancing at her every few seconds. "You know," she said casually, "it sure is nice of you as a friend to take me to the dance once in a while."

"Oh, sure," he said quickly.

"I'm really glad we're friends," Ellie said again. Then, in case he hadn't gotten the point, she added, "It's nice to be able to go out and dance with a guy once in a while without him thinking I'm interested."

She flashed Bill a friendly grin to soften the blow, and thankfully he seemed to get the hint. "Oh, yeah. Yeah, I'm glad too," he said, finally putting his eyes back on the road and keeping them there.

Phew. She let out a very small sigh of relief, glad to have avoided anything awkward, and then Bill was parking in the lot at the center.

Bill took her elbow and escorted through the door and into the din of country music and chattering voices. As Ellie's eyes adjusted, she peered urgently around the room, looking for a certain pair of sharp blue eyes.

He wasn't there.

Of course he's not here, she grumbled to herself. Why would an out-of-towner show up at their small community event? *You're being silly, Ellie,* she said mentally. *Focus on your friends.*

On her left, Bill hovered anxiously and stared at her with hopeful eyes. To the right, Ellie caught sight of her closest high school friend, Ann, accompanied by husband and daughter.

"Save me," mouthed Ellie in her direction. Luckily, the other woman noticed.

"Ellie," Ann said brightly, "why don't you come check out the desserts with me? Bill doesn't mind, does he?"

Bill shook his head, eager to please, and Ellie ducked away quickly.

"Thank you," she said in a hushed tone as they walked.

Ann laughed. "You're so welcome," she said. "I'm thinking you shouldn't accept his invitations anymore. He doesn't look like he's taking the 'just friends' thing to heart."

She sighed. "I know, but he looks so sad and hopeful every time he asks. I thought he understood, but today we're back to square one." The door opened, and she looked over hopefully, but it wasn't Calvin Barnard.

They reached the table and peered down together at brownies, sponge cakes, and pies. "Well, look at you!" Ann said, eyeing a particularly well-shaped gingersnap. "Why are you so dolled up if you didn't want attention?"

"I—" Ellie started, offended.

"I'm teasing," her friend laughed. "Relax. You look nice. It does you good to get dressed up." The door swung open again, but it was just a few of the older ladies.

When Ellie looked back at Ann, her auburn-haired friend was eyeing her suspiciously. "Okay," she said, "who is it?"

"What?" asked Ellie, still distractedly peering around.

"Elizabeth Marie, *spill*."

Ellie eyed her old friend guiltily, knowing she was busted. "Um, I don't—"

A small cluster of older women moved over, led by Kathy Timmons. "No, he is, isn't that right, Ellie?"

"I'm sorry?"

Kathy continued, looking smug about all the attention she was receiving. "There's a young man in from the big city who's clearing out Loretta Meyer's old house. He told me you were doing the renovations."

The pack of matrons around her looked at Ellie in eager fascination, and Ann raised a suspicious eyebrow.

"Oh, yes, I suppose so," responded Ellie. "It isn't official yet, but I'm working on an estimate."

Kathy lifted her chin in pride. "He asked if I'd take some of the curios and decorative items off his hands.

I can't imagine how he ended up in charge of the place."

"She was his great-aunt," cut in Ellie. Everyone spun to look at her again, and Ann's eyebrows lifted even further. She felt a self-conscious warmth creep across her face.

"He must be one of Maude Meyer's grandkids then," interjected old Mrs. Herman. "She moved off to the city way back in the '50s."

Kathy Timmons suddenly said, "Well you can ask him yourself. Look, there he is now." Ellie, whose back was to the door, spun around suddenly, ignoring Ann's knowing glance.

Chapter 5

Calvin stood just inside the door to the community center and blinked in the dim light, letting his eyes adjust from the blazing orange sunset outside. There were indeed streamers as he had guessed, and a punchbowl that looked to be filled with weak punch, and unfortunately whiny sounding country music was playing. Surprisingly, though, he didn't find it as distasteful as he'd suspected he would. There was something charming about the friendly geniality exuded by the townspeople scattered around the hall.

He let his gaze sweep the room, telling himself that he was looking for single women. There were a few who looked like they might be possible prospects, but for some reason, he kept looking. He was just trying to see all the options, he thought. He definitely didn't care if Ellie Parker was there—although it would be convenient to talk to her about the renovation.

"Excuse me," said an older woman's voice to his left. "So I hear you're renovating Loretta Meyer's old place?"

He glanced over at the speaker, a gray-haired woman who was followed by someone vaguely familiar looking.

"Uh, yes, I am," he said politely.

"Kathy here told me you were," she said, face sharp with keen interest.

Oh. Now he remembered the other woman. She was the gossipy one who owned Treasures 'n' Things. As he smiled politely at her, he was alarmed to see four or five other women drifting towards them from the dessert table.

The first speaker cleared her throat, catching his attention again before he could look closely at the pretty girl in the back of the group.

"You must be one of Maude Meyer's grandkids then?"

He nodded, still distracted by the head of expertly curled golden brown hair, but he couldn't quite see the girl's face behind a piled-up hairdo.

"You letting our Miss Ellie help you out with that renovation? She went off to college to specialize in just that," someone else said proudly.

"Well, I'm not sure—" interjected a sweetly familiar voice.

The group of busybodies parted to reveal a gorgeous woman. After a moment of staring, Calvin realized he was looking at Ellie Parker.

"Uh—" she cut off mid-sentence, blushing prettily. "What I meant to say was that I think we still need to discuss the specifics." Her wide pretty eyes narrowed into a glare at him, as she clearly remembered his earlier offense at the café.

"Yes!" said Calvin, a shade overenthusiastically. He dove forward and grabbed Ellie's arm, glad for any excuse to escape the town gossips.

The room buzzed around them, and Ellie could feel far too many curious eyes. "Sure," she said, putting on a professional tone. "Let's duck outside so we can hear one another." *And get away from all the busybodies*, she added internally.

Ellie led the way out a side door, feeling a combination of remaining irritation and a girlish nervousness. Outside it was the beautiful deep navy of late twilight, and the first stars were sparkling in the sky. Ellie took a deep breath of the clean, fresh air and turned to face the man who followed. The breeze was chilly against her bare arms, and she had to resist the urge to wrap her arms around her midriff. Instead, she stayed cold and upright, wanting to look independent and strong.

***

Calvin followed Ellie outside, half-stunned the whole time by how absurdly pretty she was. When she had been in jeans, a tee, and no makeup, the brunette had already been eye-catching, but now… Now it was hard to remember why he'd decided against making her a candidate for his inheritance marriage.

But when she turned around and eyed him coldly, he remembered why after all. *But still,* his mind said, making half-hearted excuses, *you weren't exactly nice to her.* Calvin brushed the thought away. The girl deserved an apology, and he was going to give her one, but his marriage was going to be a month- or week-long sham. He needed someone simple and easily persuaded, not a beautiful but suspicious interior designer.

"Well?" Ellie said, eyebrows knitting. With a start, he realized he had just been standing there staring down at her in the dim light.

God, judging by the way she had glared at him and tugged up her dress, she probably thought he'd been looking at her cleavage. While admittedly that view was nice, he'd actually been captivated by her beautiful face and the way the sunlight fell across her cheekbones.

A flush ran up his face at the thought, and he was glad of the dim lighting. Calvin cleared his throat. "Sorry," he said vaguely. "Um, I wanted to apologize to you for earlier."

Ellie waited. She clearly wasn't going to make this easy for him. He continued, "Clearly, what I said was out of hand. Honestly, my mouth just got ahead of my brain. I don't think you're stupid because you're from a small town or anything like that. Honest."

The woman relaxed slightly, letting her stiff shoulders loosen and looking more friendly. "I suppose I owe you an apology too," she said. "I don't think what you said was fair, but... I shouldn't have gone off on you like that."

Calvin nodded in relief. "Thank you, Ms. Parker—"

"Ellie, please," she interjected with a slight smile.

He smiled back, absurdly pleased by this request. "Thank you, Ellie. What I was going to say was that I would really, really appreciate your input on the house renovation. I hope you're willing to let me hire you still."

The slim girl stood up straighter. "Oh, sure," she said in a different tone. "I'd be a fool to turn down a customer, even if you were, well..."

"Kind of an ass?" he interjected wryly.

Ellie laughed wholeheartedly. Calvin was charmed by her full-bodied laugh, so far from the fake, girlish giggle he often got out of women. "Well, I wouldn't go that far," she said, still chuckling. "But honestly I'd be honored to help. I've always thought the house was beautiful and love the chance to work on it."

They stood there in silence for a moment, but he thought the silence seemed far more companionable than before. He was just searching for a polite way to continue the conversation when Ellie straightened up and spoke again.

"Listen," she said, "I'm probably prying, but can I ask you a question?"

"Sure," he said.

"Why are you here?" she asked, clearly curious. "No offense, but the community dance didn't seem like your kind of thing when you asked me about the singles scene."

"Well," said Calvin, but he didn't continue the sentence. He was torn between lying straight up and telling her that he was just there to apologize to her, or saying something closer to the truth. There was something about the way her brown eyes gleamed up darkly at him that appealed to his sense of integrity.

Suddenly, it occurred to him that he could use someone on his team, so to speak. He spoke carefully, giving her a very nuanced version of the truth. "My great-aunt's dying wish was that I give the women from Carterville a chance. She wanted me to go back to my family's roots. So..." He shifted uncomfortably. "I just wanted to at least consider her wishes and meet the residents of the town."

The last lie sat uneasily on his tongue, but he couldn't tell her the whole truth.

She looked unconvinced for a minute, but softened. "Huh," was all she answered. "Wouldn't have guessed that one."

Before he could say anything else, the door at his back swung open, spilling light and music out onto the parking lot.

"Ellie?" called Ann loudly.

"Uh, right here," said Ellie wryly.

"Oh, I hope I'm not interrupting," said the redhead.

"No, not at all," said Calvin in unison with Ellie's "Of course not."

Somehow he felt that their protests made them seem guilty, but Ann didn't say anything except, "Can I borrow Ellie then?"

Calvin nodded before realizing they hadn't arranged anything about the renovation. "Ellie," he said quickly as they passed back inside, "just come by the house tomorrow morning and we can work on the renovation plan."

She nodded and then disappeared through the crowd with Ann. Calvin just stood there at the door for a while, biting at the inside of his cheek and wondering if he'd revealed too much.

Chapter 6

The next morning found Calvin boxing more things up and anxiously awaiting Ellie's arrival. They hadn't set a definite time, so he knew she could show up at any minute. Furthermore, he was in the library sorting books, and he was afraid he wouldn't hear a knock at the door when she did get there.

Even though he was working on the house, his mind wasn't on the renovations. Instead, he was puzzling over Ellie's reaction last night when he had explained about trying to date women from Carterville. The interior designer was sharp, and she had seemed surprised at his motive. He wondered if she was suspicious. If she found out what his real goal was, he could lose the entire inheritance—and on top of that, he needed Ellie's help to meet women. Last night at the dance he hadn't done more than introduce himself to a few people. It had been hard to focus on being charming when a pack of curious old gossips was following him around all night.

There had been one girl that he'd danced with, blonde, pretty enough except for crooked teeth, but he couldn't remember her name. *Ellie will know.* Suddenly, he was glad that he'd told her a version of the truth. It was going to be useful to have an "inside guy" helping him meet the women of the town.

When he jogged down to the front of the house, peering out the window for the third time, he could see a plume of dust from down the road. It drifted over the bushes, covering them in a soft brown layer. *Finally*, he thought.

By the time Ellie had pulled up and parked her small green SUV, Calvin was standing at the door waiting. She got out and he said, "Thanks for coming out." Inwardly, he winced at how formal his tone sounded—he didn't need her thinking he was any more pompous than she had already accused him of being.

"Sure thing," said the brunette. He noticed that she was wearing gray cargo pants and an olive green tee. It would have looked sloppy on most people, but somehow Ellie made it look effortlessly fashionable. As he looked on, she reached into her car and pulled out a leather handyman's belt, complete with level and tape measure, which she secured around her narrow waist.

"Coffee?" he asked, leading the way inside. "I brewed extra, so there's plenty."

"Maybe later," she said. "I think I'll just try to get right to work."

"Of course," he said, nodding. "Um, where did you want to start? I was working in the library…"

Ellie shrugged with a polite smile, coming to stand next to him. "I'm going to do it room by room, so I guess we could start wherever works for you."

Calvin nodded, but he was still confused. "What exactly are you going to be doing? I'm not really clear on the process."

***

Neither was Ellie, but she didn't want to point that out to her biggest client. Still, there was no reason that renovating a larger house would be any different than working on a kitchen and living room.

"Well," she answered, "basically we go over the room piece by piece. So here"—she gestured around the kitchen—"the first question would be: do you still want this to be the kitchen? Assuming you said yes, I'd go around and discuss each thing with you: Do you like such-and-such appliance, since the linoleum needs replaced, what do you want instead, that kind of thing. Then we'd talk about color and style and from there I could bring you some specific options for the renovation."

Calvin nodded again, his blue eyes unreadable. "Sounds simple enough," he said. "Guess we might as well start in the library then."

He led the way up the stairs with Ellie close behind him. He was so quiet that she found herself chattering to fill the silence. "So you and your great-aunt, were you close?"

The man in front of her laughed wryly. "We met once."

"Oh." She wanted to ask why he'd been left the house, but that seemed impolite.

"I suppose you're wondering why she left me her house if we didn't know one another," said Calvin. She blinked at his insight and murmured in agreement. "Well, so am I," he responded.

"What are your intentions here?" she asked curiously.

"What do you mean?" Calvin spun to face her at the top of the stairs, looking oddly taken aback.

"With the house? Like do you want to set it up as a family home, vacation home, bachelor pad, or were you thinking one specific fashion design, anything like that?"

"Oh." Bizarrely, he looked relieved. "Whatever would resell best." All business again, Calvin led the way briskly down the hallway toward a door on the right.

Ellie blinked. "You're selling?"

Calvin was immediately backpedaling. "Oh, um, not necessarily. It kind of depends on how I'm feeling about the area, and work stuff... I just want it ready to sell if worst comes to worst. I'm not that picky about the design of the place."

Well, he seemed oddly defensive to her, but it was none of her business.

"So, uh, how does this work exactly?" Calvin asked, shoving his hands into his pockets.

She smiled politely at him. "Well, the first thing I need to check is what needs replacing and how big the space is. Then we can talk about what you want to do with it."

He nodded. "Okay. If that's the case, I'm going to keep working in here, as long as I'm not in the way."

Ellie just nodded again, not knowing what to say. She was more comfortable working than making small talk.

As she circled around the room, testing fabric strength, feeling wood for rot, and taking measurements, Ellie glanced at him every once in a while, but stayed quiet. She had a tendency to chatter at people when nervous, and she didn't want to irritate him by talking too much. But then she finally reached the set of shelves he knelt in front of, and maybe it was the charming way he reached up and ruffled his hair, or maybe it was just boredom with her routine task, but she couldn't keep herself from making conversation.

"What are you up to in here?"

He turned his head up to look at her, blue eyes as arresting as ever. Ellie smiled nervously down at him. He had a pink crystal flower in his hands, and when he moved it cast a small rainbow on his arm below his cuffed sleeves.

"The woman at the thrift shop—um, Kathy? Something like that—said she'd come by and buy anything she was interested in. So I figured I'd get it all ready to go for her."

"Hmm." Ellie looked at the flower in his hands again. "Anything good?"

Calvin shrugged, his broad shoulders wrinkling the cloth of his shirt momentarily. "Well, not in my estimation, but I'm not huge on decorative junk."

"Noted," she said cheerfully. "Some of that stuff does look pretty nice though, doesn't it?"

"If you like pink and sparkly, I suppose," Calvin said wryly. "But yes, mysteriously, Great-Aunt Loretta seems to have been quite well off."

"Mysteriously?"

"Sure," responded Calvin, moving on to the next item. "Didn't you ever wonder how an old, single, reclusive woman had such a big house?"

Well, the question had occurred to her, but Ellie had always assumed there was a simple explanation—

inheritance, lucrative career early in life, something like that. She said so to the New Yorker.

He shrugged. "That's the weird thing, though. Even my family doesn't seem to know where the money came from. We never knew about a job, and there couldn't have been an inheritance. My great-grandparents were a poor mining family." With the last words, he shoved a strong hand through his curly hair again, momentarily distracting her.

"Ooh," said Ellie. "I love a good mystery. Maybe we could investigate it together." She smiled cheerfully at Calvin and his wayward curls, but something in her words had made his face tighten and he didn't respond.

An awkward silence fell, so Ellie stepped past Calvin and continued with her measurements. For a long moment, the only sound in the room was the clinking of knick-knacks and the metallic sound of her extending the tape measure.

"How would you feel about letting me buy you lunch?" asked Calvin suddenly, walking up beside her.

Ellie blinked. Her first reaction was to say yes, standing there close enough to smell the warm scent of his cologne and see the stubble on his jawline. But then she remembered just how badly things had gone before. She had to keep this entirely professional.

"I don't know how professional it would be to let you finance my lunches," she said, trying to laugh it off casually.

"Well, we could keep it totally separate from the work we're doing," he said. "It's just that I haven't had time to make any friends, but I'd really love if someone could show me around Carterville so I can start getting to know the town and the people. And I'd like to make up for the last lunch."

She softened at his explanation. It was nice to see him taking an interest in local culture, instead of dismissing their town as rustic and boring. And Ellie truly did love this little town—as soon as he mentioned wanting to get to know it, she immediately thought of five or six places he *had* to see.

"Well... Maybe if I paid for my own food?"

***

Calvin watched Ellie flash him a heart-stopping smile as she acquiesced to his request and sucked in a slow, steadying breath. It was going to be difficult to stay away from this beautiful woman, but she wasn't the kind of girl you temporarily married and then ditched once a check paid out.

No, Ellie Parker was the kind of strong, beautiful, intelligent woman—with a good sense of humor to boot—that he'd consider dating seriously if she lived in New York and had a similar lifestyle to him. But as things were, she was a small-town girl with plans and a career of her own, not to mention a woman who was already questioning the circumstances of his great-aunt's inheritance. Ellie was off-limits for his temporary marriage. But she could still help Calvin succeed in his mission to marry.

He acquiesced to her suggestion for lunch, which was pasta at some American/Italian combo place, and let her drive him down in her little SUV. Somehow, he thought, the car suited her. It was petite and kind of cute, but it was also really functional and capable of getting the job done.

"You know," he said once they were inside the car, trying to sound casual, "I just realized I danced with someone at the community dance and I don't even know her name."

Ellie glanced at him before looking back at the road. "The blonde? Dana Cartwright, maybe?"

"Yes, blonde," he said.

"Yellow dress? Um, crooked teeth?" Ellie sounded a little embarrassed at using the last descriptor, which Calvin found surprisingly endearing.

He hid a smile. "Yes, that's her."

"Definitely Dana," Ellie said. Then, after a pause: "Why, are you interested in her?"

The truth was that he wasn't at all interested in Dana as an actual partner, but he was *very* interested in her as a candidate for his temporary marriage. Leaving it noncommittal, he just shrugged. "I just figured I should at least find out her name in case I see her around."

When he looked at Ellie again, she was giving him a very suspicious look, so he decided to push back. "Speaking of, who was that man *you* were dancing with?"

Ellie went a satisfying shade of pink. "Oh, that's just old Bill Carlisle," she said, waving a hand to dismiss the question while keeping her eyes locked on the road.

Aha. Ellie was off-limits for more reasons than one, judging by her reaction. "You guys make a handsome couple," Calvin said. He was lying—Ellie deserved better than that redneck—but she didn't need to know that.

"Oh no, we aren't a couple!" she exclaimed abruptly. "Just friends. Absolutely just friends"—and then she looked over at Calvin again and went from pink to bright red.

Interesting. Calvin mentally filed away her reaction for later analysis and changed topics, trying to ignore the pretty glow her flushed cheeks gave her complexion as they pulled into the parking lot of their destination.

The restaurant was cute, and his plate of ravioli was downright delicious. Throughout the meal, Ellie chattered in a pleasant way, talking about the "quality woodwork" in the house, the beautiful views outside, and the kinds of clients she was currently working with at the store. Thankfully, she didn't go back to the topic of Great-Aunt Loretta's money or his dance partner—Calvin didn't know if he could continue to lie directly to Ellie. A funny anecdote about an old man who insisted that she order in a dishwasher that had twist knobs instead of "those funky newfangled electric buttons" had Calvin still laughing as he asked their teenaged waiter for the check.

He still hadn't thought of a way to get Ellie to introduce him to single women, but he figured meeting women would follow naturally as he spent time out and around in town. In fact, his idea was proved right as they stood to leave, because two women who were having lunch a few tables over waved brightly, and Ellie led Calvin over to say hi.

"Jane, Mal, haven't seen you in a bit!"

Both women smiled politely. Calvin noticed a wedding ring on the finger of the brunette who sat closer to them, but the woman next to her had unembellished hands.

The presumably single one sat up and grinned in a direct way at both Calvin and Ellie. "Hey, honey!" she said, brushing tight black curls away from her plump-but-pretty face. "Who is this?"

Calvin saw Ellie's round cheeks go a little bit pink at the openly curious tone, but her voice didn't waver at all. "Mallory, this is Calvin—I'm working with him to remodel Miss Loretta Meyer's old house."

"Pleasure," purred Mallory, leaning across the table to shake his hand. She had a limp grip, but Calvin smiled at her anyway.

"And this is Jane," Ellie said, with a nod to the married woman. "We all three went to high school together."

"Nice to meet you," Jane said in a sweet, high-pitched voice. She didn't bother shaking his hand.

"Carterville natives, eh?" said Calvin, trying to be pleasant.

"Oh, su-ure," said Mallory, still batting her eyelashes at him. His first impulse was to quickly back away and disengage, but then he remembered that this was exactly the kind of girl he was looking for—quick and easy marriage, no guilt over near-instant divorce. In contrast, Jane had stopped listening in favor of some game on her cellphone. But he was certain neither woman would ever be suspicious about what his great-aunt had left him or his intentions with women, unlike Ellie.

"Well, anyway," said Ellie, "we ought to get back to work. Nice seeing you two!"

Put Mallory on the list of potentials, Calvin noted to himself as he followed Ellie out of the restaurant.

"So, good friends of yours?" he asked his companion. He wanted a little bit of information, like whether or not Mallory was actually single.

Ellie snorted loudly, before clearly remembering whom she was with and trying to regain her composure. "Ah, not exactly," she murmured.

Calvin raised his eyebrows. "What exactly, then?"

"Well…" Ellie seemed to ponder the question for a minute as she led the way back to the car. "My high school class was small enough that we're all kind of friends, because we're all neighbors. But back in the day those two weren't exactly my favorite people."

"Back in the day?" He snorted. "You act as though you're an ancient old woman."

Ellie smiled at this as she climbed into the car and started it up. "It feels like it sometimes. I've changed so much since then." There was an oddly serious note to her voice, and Calvin wondered briefly what she had experienced to make her sound so sad.

But before he could find a way to politely ask, the pretty brunette had shaken off whatever hung on her mind and was acting cheerful again. "Okay, now if you want the real Carterville experience, we have to get ice cream at Rich's and walk in the park while we eat it!" A note of childlike glee had entered her voice, and Calvin found himself unable to say no.

In fact, as he followed her to Rich's, which turned out to be a small roadside stand next to the park, and then along the wending path between the leafy trees, Calvin forgot about the will and the mystery of his great-aunt's money and his intent to find a wife. For a few moments, he didn't think of anything but the cold mint chocolate chip ice cream against his tongue, the fresh smell of the cool breeze, and the pretty smile that Ellie Parker flashed up at him every so often.

Chapter 7

Two weeks later, Ellie was singing along cheerfully in the car on the way out of the Parker Home Design parking lot.

The renovation of Calvin's house was going brilliantly, a thought that made her feel quite proud. Together, they had developed a plan of action for almost every room in the house, and in a few days she had workers coming in with a truck to take all the furniture to her store for reupholstering. She had been putting in half days at the shop, since honestly she didn't need to do eight hours of work a day with the small amount of business they had, and it was doing her good to have a big project to focus on.

And Calvin… Well, the handsome New Yorker had been surprisingly good company for the last two weeks. When she was at work in the house, she only saw him every hour or two, when she checked in to get his input on room design. But it was somehow comforting just to hear him humming away in whatever room he was packing as she walked by from room to room, taking dozens of measurements and setting up preliminary design sketches for his approval.

Best of all, though, were their lunches together every few days. Not only did she enjoy the time with Calvin, but Ellie also felt like she was falling in love with her hometown all over again. Pointing out the good places to Calvin made her appreciate the small community even more.

Hmm, where to go today? She tapped her lip thoughtfully as she drove up the highway and the dirt road. It struck her that she had stopped thinking of the house as Miss Meyer's place, and started thinking of it as Calvin's, which drew an unbidden smile from her lips. However, that still didn't answer the question of lunch. They had hit up all the good restaurants in town already—Carterville was small, after all. But for some reason Ellie couldn't bring herself to say Calvin had seen everything. She had to admit that she didn't want to stop having lunch with him. In fact, she was coming out to his house far more often than she needed to just so she could have more of his company.

As she stared at the passing trees, inspiration struck. *Of course!* One of the best things in Carterville wasn't a store or anything manmade, but the natural surroundings themselves.

When she pulled up alongside Calvin's rental car and parked, Ellie swung open the door and then hesitated. Without stopping to question her behavior, she opened her glove box and rummaged around for a minute before emerging with an old tube of soft pink lipstick. She swiped a light coat of it on, using her rearview mirror to check the application, and then grinned at herself before getting out of the car and grabbing her equipment. She had to admit she could have done a lot of the sketches and product selection in her office, but for some reason she preferred to be near Calvin.

Ellie tapped on the thick wooden door of the purple house, but when there was no answer she went ahead and swung it open.

"Helloooo?" she called cheerfully. "I brought the upholstery samples like we talked about!"

"Hi!" called Calvin's familiar deep voice. He wasn't visible, but she could hear that he was just in the next room to the left, the living room.

"Hi!" said Ellie, smiling a little. "So, I had an idea for lunch! What do you think of—" She stopped abruptly as she crossed into the other room and saw Calvin adding a box to a mountain of the things. "Whoa."

Peering around his armload, Calvin grinned cheekily, blue eyes crinkling up nicely. "Impressed? I've been working hard all morning."

Ellie looked around, taking in the house. Except for furniture, it was dead empty. No décor remained on the walls other than a few decorative mirrors, all the shelves stood empty, the drawers hung open, and the tables were cleared. "I'm definitely impressed," she said. Although Calvin had been boxing things up the whole time she'd been working, he hadn't been putting that much effort in. Ellie often found him paging through books instead of boxing them, or sitting back and looking at curios instead of sorting. But clearly, this morning he had decided to make up for lost time. "Why the sudden effort?"

He made a mock-offended face. "Why, Miss Parker," he said, putting on a fake accent, "I'm surprised at you. I put effort into *everything* I do."

She hid a smile at his drawl and waited for him to finish putting down the boxes and explain himself.

Finally, Calvin settled everything and stood, brushing his hands against his khakis. "Honestly," he said, "I had been going slower and slower because I was looking at things. And as much as I wanted to…"

"To get to know your great-aunt?" Ellie guessed softly.

He nodded tightly, not saying anything for a moment. "Yeah, basically. As much as I wanted that, staring at all her pretty things wasn't helping me understand her any more. It was just slowing me down. I woke up this morning and realized I was never going to finish if I kept trying to be an archaeologist." He worked his throat roughly. "This used to be her house, and these things used to matter to her—but even if I make them all matter to me, she is gone anyway. It's just my house now. I feel guilty for intruding, though."

Recognizing the familiar pain of grief and loss on his face, Ellie stepped to Calvin and put a soft hand on his shoulder. "I'm sure she would understand."

Calvin murmured in agreement, and for one short moment they stood together quietly. Suddenly, Ellie remembered her hand was still on his shoulder, feeling the heat of his skin through the fabric, and she stepped back abruptly.

"Sorry," said Calvin, shaking his head with a bemused expression like he was emerging from underwater. "Anyway, point of that whole anecdote is this morning I woke up motivated, so I called up Kathy at Treasures 'n' Things and told her tomorrow was the day, and the rest is history." He gestured at the boxes.

"Sounds great," said Ellie. "Oh! I had a really good idea for lunch, by the way."

"What idea is that?"

"Well, I was thinking we ought to have a picnic! We could make our food here or pick up sandwiches to go from Susie's. That's the place that we went on the first day... the, well, you remember." Ellie anxiously wondered what Calvin was thinking—with him behind her, she couldn't even see his facial expressions.

He snorted. "I do remember. The place where I was a pompous jerk."

"Well, I wasn't going to be winning Miss Congeniality for that either," Ellie laughed.

"A picnic sounds wonderful!" he continued. "Are there any especially nice places to picnic at?"

She paused in the hallway, idea suddenly sparking. Calvin came to stand beside her, and she turned to smile up into his blue eyes as she talked. "Oh, come to think of it! You haven't seen the falls yet! They're beautiful this time of year. The trailhead is actually just up this road—Oh." Her enthusiasm suddenly waned. "We probably shouldn't be taking a long lunch in the middle of trying to pack in a hurry."

Honestly, he really couldn't spare any time—and a walk to a rural waterfall would not help him track down a wife. Other than one date with Dana Cartwright—which had been totally unbearable, even for the sake of $10 million—Calvin had barely seen anyone but Ellie. But still... She looked so sad, like a puppy or something, and he simply couldn't tell her no.

"Okay," he said, "what about this? Why don't we go the day the movers come out with the new furniture? I just have to finish up a storage room and the master bedroom to get everything cleared out—though I might have gotten ahead of myself with that." He crinkled his face up in worry.

A smile bloomed over Ellie's pretty heart-shaped face, and Calvin felt his heart warm. "That sounds perfect," she said. "Listen, do you need help? I could probably take a break to help you." For a second, she felt guilty for even making the offer—Ellie had been closing up the shop far more often than she needed to, and helping with Calvin's chores was *definitely* not her job. But she was enjoying herself here at the house with him.

"Really? That would be great!" He dragged his eyes off her and started walking up the stairs. *She's off limits,* he reminded himself. *You're not going to marry her for the sake of money, and you sure aren't going to date her and then suddenly marry another woman.* Aloud, he said, "Why don't we start here with this storage room? As far as I can tell it was just used as some kind of junk disposal—there are heaps of old boxes that don't seem organized in any way."

Ellie seemed frozen in some kind of stupefied horror at the heap of decaying boxes before them, but when she said, "Wow," in a hushed tone, he realized her look was something more like excitement.

"I've already pulled a few things out, but as you can see, there's a lot left to do. I've been sorting everything into new boxes since these old ones are literally falling apart. I'll bring up some more collapsed boxes."

When he returned with the boxes, Ellie was into the pile up to her elbows and clutching a handful of dusty jewelry, a music box, and some sort of ornate wall ornament. "Some of this stuff is *beautiful*," she said, turning to him with shining eyes. He hid a smile when he saw a big smudge of dust across her nose.

"Well, if you want, you could keep it. Anything, really."

She blushed. "Oh no, I couldn't." But he saw the longing look she gave one particular opal ring as she tucked the armload into a fresh box. When she handed him the filled box and he carried it downstairs, Calvin reached in and fished around for that ring. He hardly knew what he was doing, but he pulled it out—and he had to admit, shining in the light from the window, it was pretty—and tucked it away in his pocket.

For a few long hours, they worked diligently from different edges of the room. Ellie was quiet the whole time, but he could see her messy ponytail bobbing as she looked through things, and once in a while she made a happy little humming noise. Calvin was glad to have her company. He hoped he wasn't taking her away from anything too important—but since he was her main client and he didn't care, he doubted there would be customer complaints.

Finally, he stood and stepped cautiously between boxes to get to Ellie. She was sitting cross-legged, sorting out two different piles of clothing, and instead of standing to talk to him she just craned her neck upward and smiled. She was staggeringly beautiful, even with dust smudged on her face.

"Lunch time?" he asked.

"Oh, yes please," said Ellie with a laugh. She tucked a wayward strand of hair behind her ear before continuing, "I'm dying. I didn't want to wimp out if you weren't though."

Calvin chuckled. "Same here. Come on, let's go grab something." He took a step back. The petite woman before him pushed herself up to do the same, but her foot caught on something with a loud thump and she started to topple over. Calvin reached to catch her without thinking about it, but she managed to correct her balance herself, leaving him standing there with outstretched arms, feeling stupid.

"Ouch," she said, frowning down at her foot. "That felt heavier than another cardboard box." He watched as she carefully lifted the box off whatever she had kicked and set it to the side. "Oh, how beautiful!"

Calvin craned his head over to see what the petite woman was looking at. Before them sat a dusty wooden trunk, painted with an intricate green and gold design. A small gold lock was clipped to the front of it, but a key was already inserted. "Is anything inside it?" he asked.

"Well, let's see." Ellie adeptly undid the lock, flipped back two gold-colored clasps, and swung the lid open. The sound was accompanied by the creak of an old hinge, but it moved easily enough. "It's all wrapped in tissue," she murmured.

Calvin watched as Ellie carefully unfolded old, crackly paper to reveal two photographs. She handed them over to Calvin, and his breath caught in his throat at the unexpected sight of his mother's face. She was young in the posed portrait, and holding a small, dark-headed toddler on her hip that Calvin knew must be him. Feeling emotional, he flipped to the photo behind it, and found a stiff-looking posed portrait of a family. The sepia sheet showed a handsome man with round glasses and side-combed hair next to a woman with a curled bob. On her lap sat a serious looking child in a dress. Calvin didn't really recognize any of them. He flipped it over to the back, squinting at spidery handwriting.

John, Maude, & A.

His eyes widened and he hurriedly turned it to see the front again. John and Maude were his mother's parents, which meant "A" was Ann. This photo had his mom in it as well. It must have been taken before Aunt Sheila was born, he mused.

"What is it?" asked Ellie, her soft voice breaking his reverie. "You looked startled."

Calvin cleared his throat quickly. "It's old pictures of my family, actually," he said. "My grandparents when my mom was a baby, and a photo of me and my mom."

"Oh, that's so sweet that your great-aunt had them," Ellie said. "I bet your family will be glad to see them."

His throat tightened again, and he cleared it more forcefully. "My Aunt Sheila will," he said. "But my mom isn't around. She died when I was a teenager."

Ellie looked totally stricken, dark eyes going wide and shimmering with a hint of tears. "I'm so sorry," she said, putting a slim hand on his shoulder. "I lost my dad recently. I know it's tough." With her this close, Calvin could smell the sweet scent of Ellie's perfume or soap.

He shrugged, trying to shake off his sudden grief. "I've had a while to get used to it."

With a slow nod, Ellie reached to peer at the picture in his hand. "So this is you?" she asked, pointing to the toddler. When he nodded, she laughed. "Cute kid." Then, reaching to hand the photo back, she muttered, "It figures." Calvin was pretty sure he hadn't been supposed to hear that part, so he didn't acknowledge it.

Ellie reached into the trunk again, ponytail swinging as she pulled out another tissue-wrapped packet. Calvin stood next to her, peering down in curiosity. This one contained another black-and-white photo and a faded, yellowed newspaper clipping. She handed them to Calvin. "Who's this one?" she asked.

But Calvin didn't know, and there was no label on the back. He sat the picture of the mystery man aside for a moment to look at the newspaper clipping instead. Craning his neck down at the chest was getting uncomfortable, so he sat down on the floor cross-legged next to Ellie.

"Carterville New Vacation Destination"

He skimmed the small article for a moment, trying to figure out why it had been saved. "Talbot family has taken mountain home," "Cordelia, Edward, and sons Edward Jr. and Tommy, owners of a logging dynasty," "others from growing city of Portland expected to follow," "new age of tourism for the Carterville area." By the time he reached the cutoff at the bottom, "Article Continues on Page 3," he wasn't any closer to understanding why it had been saved.

"Anything else?" asked Calvin.

"Just these," said Ellie. She reached into the bottom of the trunk and pulled out two folded pieces of fabric. When shaken out, the top piece revealed itself to be a very small pink-striped blanket, while the bottom was a faded lavender dress, complete with puff shoulders and pointed collar. It looked old, but Calvin couldn't have said when the style dated from. "Pretty," Ellie murmured. "I wonder what they were for."

He didn't know. Clearly these things in the trunk had been important to his great-aunt, but Calvin had no idea *why*. Frustration washed over him. The woman who had left him all of her belongings and money was a huge mystery, and he wanted answers—but his only resource was his Aunt Sheila, and even she hadn't known where the money had come from.

Ellie looked delicate and vulnerable as she sat there on the floor, biting at her lip, clearly deep in thought. Calvin was suddenly hyperaware of his proximity to her—their shoulders almost brushed with every breath, and his knee was bumped up against her smaller one. He could see her long, dark eyelashes and smell the floral scent of her perfume as she looked down at the bundle of fabric.

A desire to be even closer consumed him momentarily. Without conscious decision, he felt himself leaning in as though he was going to kiss Ellie. She looked at him silently, neither moving forward nor back, but her eyes shone up at him and he thought he saw her full pink lips part slightly.

But right then he remembered what he had decided. *She's off-limits.* Calvin abruptly cleared his throat and sat up straight.

"Um…" His mind raced trying to come up with a conversation topic that would break the awkward silence. "So, ready for lunch?"

"Great!" said Ellie, turning red and jumping up. "I mean, yeah. Lunch sounds great." He could tell she wanted to look anywhere but at him as she brushed invisible dust of her pants and headed toward the door. Calvin winced, realizing that it had looked like a complete rejection on his part. If only he could explain that he *did* want to kiss her.

After delicious sandwiches at Susie's, Calvin was standing outside waiting for Ellie to finish in the bathroom.

"Fancy seeing you here!" called a chirpy female voice. He didn't recognize it, so he spun slowly, not sure the words were meant for him. A little red sedan had pulled up behind him in the parking lot, and the dark-haired woman from a few days earlier—Mallory—was waving coyly at him from the driver's seat.

She had her dark hair tucked up into a fancy bun, and heavy makeup on, but Calvin was amused to realize she still wasn't as pretty as Ellie. He strolled over toward her window when it became obvious that she wanted to chat, thinking again of his imaginary "potential wife" list.

"Hi," he said noncommittally.

Mallory smiled in an ingratiating manner. "*So* nice to see you," she said. "What are you doing in town?"

"Ellie has been showing me around on our lunch breaks."

The woman's nose wrinkled for a minute, but she mastered her expression quickly. "Aw, that's so sweet of her. Tell you what—why don't I give you my phone number and I can show you a few of my favorite places too?"

If Calvin hadn't been looking for a girl just like her, he would have laughed at the obviousness of her ploy. But as it was, he just smiled and said, "Sure." She was playing right into his plans, and he had no compunctions about taking advantage of it. He was willing to bet that if he did marry her, she wouldn't even complain about the pretense when he gave her a decent chunk of the money after the whole thing went through.

Mallory took his phone from him and tap-tapped her number into the contact screen. When he took it back, he was amused to see that she'd programmed her name as "Mal XOXO."

"So, I have to ask," she said with a high-pitched laugh, "is Ellie just working for you? Or..." She trailed off suggestively.

Calvin frowned a little bit. "She's just—We're friends." With some surprise, he realized that it should have been true—but it wasn't. He felt *far* more strongly about Ellie than he did about a friend. He wanted to spend every minute of every day with her, and hold her and kiss her and hear her secrets and dreams. *He had fallen hard for Ellie Parker.* The thought hit him like a punch in the stomach.

"Well," said the woman before him, interrupting his racing thoughts, "how sweet! I'm sure she could use more friends."

Before he could fully process the barb, Mallory was saying, "Bye for now and do call me!" and pulling back out of the parking lot.

What an unpleasant woman, he thought. And then he thought, *but she is absolutely perfect for meeting the conditions of my great-aunt's will.* He made sure the phone number had saved properly.

Just then, Ellie emerged, and he brushed away the thoughts and focused on the packing they had left to do.

They chatted easily on the drive back up the hill, and once inside they were able to quickly finish clearing the storage room. Everything was downstairs except that mysterious wooden chest, which Calvin had moved inside the bedroom where he'd been sleeping for later perusal.

Reluctantly, Calvin sent Ellie home. As much as he was enjoying her company, he knew that she needed to rest and do her own job. And furthermore, with every extra minute he spent in her company she was starting to win him over more, and he didn't need that complication in his life.

Calvin was feeling more optimistic with the end in sight. *Now,* he thought as he surveyed the pile of boxes, *just to clean up the master bedroom and hope that Kathy will buy it all.*

Instead of heading into his great-aunt's bedroom, though, Calvin poured himself a glass of red wine and sat down with the decorative chest again. Picture of him and his mom, picture of his mom and her parents, picture of mystery man, random newspaper article, blanket, and dress. It just didn't add up. Maybe he was wrong, but Calvin couldn't shake the feeling that the items in this chest had had some special importance to Loretta Meyer.

Chapter 8

When Ellie showed up at the house the next morning, she was still mulling over yesterday in her head. For a moment when they were cleaning out the storage room, she could have sworn that Calvin had been about to kiss her. Her heart had sped up until it was whirring like a small hummingbird, and she had finally had to admit to herself that she had fallen desperately for Calvin. Everything she'd wanted had been right there at hand—but then he hadn't done it.

Ellie sighed and pushed open the door to the mansion. It was quite obvious that whatever feelings she'd been harboring were unrequited. Inside, she could see that the box pile had continued to grow while she was gone. She followed the sounds of shuffling upstairs and found Calvin's tall frame wedged into a small closet, stuffing clothing into a box.

The dust in the air made her sneeze, and Calvin spun at the sound, poking his head out of the door. "Hi," he said sheepishly.

"Sorry to startle you," Ellie said, trying to hide her amused smile. "I knocked but you didn't answer, so I figured you were up here somewhere."

"Yeah," he said. "I woke up and I felt bad about taking advantage of you to do my packing, so I decided to get right to work here in Great-Aunt Loretta's room."

She felt herself soften at this. "I don't mind helping. That's what friends are for."

Quiet reigned for a moment and she spoke again, awkwardly toying with the strings of her sweatshirt hood. "We are friends, right?"

"Of course," said Calvin, coming to stand next to her with a warm smile. Light from the window flashed in his blue eyes, and Ellie thought wistfully for the millionth time about how handsome he was. For a moment, he looked at her quietly, but then he cleared his throat and kept talking. "So since I'm done here, feel free to work on whatever you need to. I'm just going to finish in here and tidy things a little more. That way Kathy can look through them easily."

"Oh, that sounds great," said Ellie.

But the problem was that it didn't. She didn't want to go back to work in a different room. She wanted to spend another day working and laughing alongside Calvin. Biting her lip fretfully, she peered around the room. "You know, I could do the measurements in here," she offered, trying to sound casual. *Maybe it was stupid to go pining after some stockbroker from a big city across the country, but he had said himself that he wanted to give the women of Carterville a chance. Maybe he would change his mind about her.*

"Sure," he said over his shoulder, heading back over to the closet. "You must be about done with the other rooms, right?"

"Great!" answered Ellie, and this time she really meant it. "I am pretty much done with the things I can do alone—after this I'll hire a few laborers to come in and start taking out the old curtains, while we finalize the designs for each space. Then we bring in movers to take the old furniture out, tear up the carpets, replace them, and repaint the walls. And then you'll have your new stylish house."

Calvin just smiled and nodded before ducking back into the closet.

As he started filling boxes again, she stretched and cracked her knuckles, looking around at the room. She realized that she'd forgotten her measurement tools in the car, so after a quick jog downstairs, she was back with trusty tool belt and notepad. This time, Calvin wasn't in the room to absorb her attention, so she had a chance to really take in the space. Loretta Meyer had been an enigma to the townspeople of Carterville the entire time Ellie was growing up, and it was strange to stand inside the woman's inner sanctum.

Ellie walked over to the table beside the bed, trying to imagine a woman that neither she nor Calvin had ever really met living in this space. "Hey," she called to Calvin, "did you ever figure anything out about the contents of that decorative chest?"

"Nope," he said, voice muffled in the closet. "Other than the pictures of my family, I have no idea what those things are or why she had them. Guess even my reclusive great-aunt had a life and secrets of her own."

For some reason, that thought made Ellie smile. It was comforting to think that even Loretta Meyer, who never left her house, could have had secrets and loves and dreams. "I guess even the simplest seeming life," she mused out loud, "must have its own moments of joy and sorrow."

Calvin poked his head out again, brow furrowed. "You sound really serious suddenly."

Ellie blushed, caught in her moment of introspection. "I guess I relate a little bit to your great-aunt," she said. "It's comforting to think that even she had things in her life that we don't know about."

He quirked his head. "What do you possibly mean? You're young and vibrant and outgoing—hardly an old recluse."

"Well," she said honestly, "I don't see much in my future except my same old life in Carterville. I already know everyone here, so it's not like I'm going to run into anyone and have a Cinderella story. I'll probably grow old here with the same people, doing the same things at the family business." *In fact,* she added to herself, *you're the only guy around here I've even been interested in since high school… and now I've fallen hard for you and you don't seem to be interested.*

She thought she saw pity on his face, so she hurried to correct her statement. "It's not that I mind, honestly. I *chose* to come home and take over the business when my dad died, and I love this town. It's just that sometimes it seems a terribly simple life." Ellie cut off abruptly, feeling that she was oversharing. She wasn't sure why she had been so honest with Calvin Barnard, but for some reason she felt a need for him to really understand and know her.

"Was that always your plan?" he asked. "To take over your dad's business, I mean."

Ellie sighed, taken back to long-forgotten dreams. "Maybe not exactly. I used to have all these plans of turning the shop into a full fancy showroom, like IKEA, and working with my dad to offer design consultation and remodel—kind of like I'm doing here with you actually. I was going to move to Portland and set up my own interior design service

91

and consult for my dad on the side. But then he got sick and, well, life intervened, I guess."

"It has a habit of doing that," Calvin said. The gentle sound of his deep voice rolled comfortably over her, and she was painfully glad to see that he didn't think she was foolish for coming home to Carterville.

He tried to think of something else to say, but right then the phone in his pocket began vibrating. He didn't recognize the number that flashed on the screen as he slid to accept the call.

"Hello?"

"Hello, Mr. Barnard. This is Walter Greenfeld."

"Oh!" He glanced quickly at Ellie, who was looking at him curiously. "Uh, hold on just a minute." Calvin slipped out the door and jogged downstairs. There was no way he wanted Ellie overhearing any of this.

In the kitchen, he started talking again quietly. "Hi, Mr. Greenfeld. Sorry about that. What can I do for you?"

"I just wanted to let you know that one of our associates will be available at the Carterville office this Thursday and Friday. We have someone available there two days of every month. If you need any legal advice regarding the will provisions or are ready to take steps forward, this is your chance."

"Thank you for letting me know," murmured Calvin. "I'm not really at a point for any of that, but I appreciate it." He glanced toward the doorway, glad to see no sign of Ellie. A sick, guilty feeling was spreading through the pit of his stomach as the reminder of the encroaching deadline hit him like a cold splash of water.

"Of course," said the lawyer gruffly. "Just a friendly reminder then that you are nearly halfway to the deadline." His voice softened. "Not that you are required to act, of course."

"Yeah," Calvin said tightly. "Thank you." He looked nervously around again, but the room was empty. "I have to go. I'll see your associate if I have any questions."

Without waiting for a response, he ended the call. He knew he was being unnecessarily rude, especially when the elderly lawyer had been nothing but kind, but the call was a rough awakening. Every day he spent puttering around the house and wasting time with Ellie was a day closer to losing $10 million.

He was just standing there pondering things when Ellie came running down the stairs.

"Calvin!" she called, sounding breathless and excited. "Calvin! Have you been in the attic?"

What? She flew around the corner, coming to an abrupt stop before him. "The attic! Look!" Her petite arms were loaded with a dusty cardboard box, packed with leather-bound books, and she looked more beautiful than ever. Calvin's heart twinged at the sight of her excited face.

"What is it?"

"They're *diaries*!" she said. "They're your great-aunt's diaries! This could solve the mystery! And there are more boxes up there!"

He forgot his worries about the will and peered excitedly into the box. "Seriously?"

"Yes, look!" Ellie plopped right down on the kitchen floor and tugged a book out of the box. She opened to a ribbon-marked page and said, "Listen to this one! 'It seems so strange to know that I will never see you again. We haven't been in contact in years, but I supposed I still hoped that you would change your mind and come back into my life. To hear today that you are gone… it has shaken me. I hope you have found peace and happiness at last, even if we couldn't have it together. You gave me more than I could ever thank you for, and I wish I would have swallowed my pride enough to tell you.'" She looked up at him with shining eyes and patted the floor next to her. "See! Isn't it terribly romantic and sad?"

Calvin sat, looking sharply at the books. *Answers at last.* He only hoped they didn't reveal more to Ellie than he had planned on. "You said they were in the attic?" he asked. "I didn't know there was an attic."

"It's more of a crawlspace, really," she answered absently, flipping through the diary. "I noticed the roof panel in the library when I moved a shelf."

He frowned at her, suddenly concerned. "You shouldn't be moving furniture around on your own. You could hurt yourself." He didn't ask himself why he cared so much, but Ellie didn't even notice, just waving an absent hand at him as she continued reading.

"These are so fascinating," she breathed. "Your great-aunt didn't write a diary entry every day by any means, but there's so much here. There were two more boxes up in the crawlspace. Listen! 'Rainy, gloomy day today. Missing you and her more than ever. Too many secrets are bad for the soul, I suppose. Wish I had known this when I agreed to Maude's last wishes.' How mysterious!"

Calvin suddenly focused entirely on the book. "Maude's last wishes? Maude was my grandmother. What were her last wishes?"

Ellie shrugged. "It doesn't say here, but I bet it would in one of these! Oh, Calvin, can we read them all? Do you mind?" Her dark eyes shone earnestly at him.

He didn't know. "It feels invasive, but…" *But he wanted answers.*

"Oh," said Ellie, "about that! These are in chronological order, I think, and the last one here was dated only a few years ago." She grabbed the last book and flipped to the back. "See? 'This volume is full, and I find the arthritis in my hands pains me more and more when I write. It's foolish to hurt myself writing to you when you're no longer here. I'd burn these notebooks, but I can't bear to have so much of my life go unknown. For now I'll hide this away with its companion volumes from the many years, and maybe take them down to read once in a while if I feel too alone.' So doesn't it sound as though she wouldn't have minded?"

That was close enough to permission for him. He took the volume from Ellie's slim hands and peered down in fascination at the spidery handwriting that covered the page. It was the same as the writing on the pictures in the old wooden chest, although perhaps shakier.

He was about to say yes, but a knock at the door echoed through the house. He and Ellie both jumped up, nearly colliding with one another, and she leaned down to grab the box, looking flustered.

"*Shoot*," he said. "That'll be Kathy. Look, Ellie, I'd love to read those… but later?"

The brunette nodded and scurried back toward the stairs with the box as he strode over to the door.

At some point while Calvin watched Kathy Timmons dig through all his boxes, Ellie made her exit. She was entirely cool and professional as she strode out the door, clutching her clipboard and casually waving.

"I'll see you tomorrow, Mr. Barnard," she said. He wondered why she was acting so aloof, but maybe it had something to do with the extra presence in the house. People in Carterville were certainly prone to gossip, and maybe Ellie wanted to avoid being the target of that.

When the door close, he shifted his attention back to the older woman who knelt before him. She was certainly taking her time about making a decision, though she already had a growing pile of trinkets by the door.

The afternoon dragged on, and Kathy still wasn't done perusing. Calvin gave up on supervising and went into the kitchen to make himself lunch, with a reminder to Kathy to find him if she had any questions. When his meal was done, he fidgeted, full of boredom and nervous energy. He had an overpowering urge to read his great-aunt's diaries immediately—but Ellie had been so curious and he didn't want her to feel left out.

Instead he turned his attention to the call from Mr. Greenfeld. *How was the time halfway over?* It occurred to him that soon he would have to go back to New York and back to his job. At first, he had been impatient for his return, but now his old life seemed totally foreign. How could he just leave Carterville behind? How could he leave *Ellie*?

A sudden idea occurred to him. With the inheritance money, he would be able to quit his job. "I could quit my job and move here," he said out loud, mouth hanging open at the sheer audacity of the idea.

"Did you say something in there?" called Kathy Timmons from the other room.

Oops. "No, sorry!" called Calvin hurriedly. "Just talking to myself!"

He sat down heavily in a chair. If he moved here, he could see Ellie whenever he wanted. He could enjoy the fruits of remodeling his house, and take all the time in the world to read his great-aunt's diaries. Calvin realized that, much to his astonishment, he didn't want to go back to New York. Sure, he would miss his friends, but Carterville felt more like home each day.

There was just one problem. The only way to get the money was to get married, and fast. He reached for his phone and tapped an entry in the address book.

Chapter 9

As expected, when the phone rang through to "Mal XOXO" she had quickly agreed to the idea of a date with Calvin. In fact, she hadn't even waited for him to mention a day or time—instead, Mallory had immediately offered to meet him at the pub that night. He had agreed, and once Kathy Timmons had finally left, taking close to 10 boxes and paying him generously, he had gotten dressed quickly.

Calvin was glad that Mallory still seemed aggressively interested in him. He strode into the bar at 8:17, two minutes late for their date, and caught sight of the woman immediately.

The few other people in the bar wore jeans and T-shirts, but not Mallory. No, she was in a skin-tight, lime-green dress, so short that it barely covered her backside, and high heels that must have been five inches tall. Her black curls tumbled down the open back of her dress, and when she spun and waved to Calvin from the bar, he was pretty sure he could see fake eyelashes on her eyelids.

"Honey, I'm *so* glad you called me," she purred as he sat down.

"Me too, Mallory," Calvin said, which was a complete lie. He missed Ellie's easygoing charm and natural beauty.

"Oh, do call me Mal." The bartender handed her a martini, and the curvaceous woman held it in one hand while resting her head flirtatiously against the other. "I have to tell you," she said, "we don't see guys like you in Carterville often. Powerful, hard-working, successful, stylish, well-off…"

She didn't say "rich," but she might as well have. Calvin nearly laughed aloud. Maybe this was going to be easier than he thought. "It is a pretty small town," he said noncommittally.

"So tell me, what are you doing hanging around here?" She batted her eyelashes.

Perfect. She was playing right into his hands. Calvin took a breath and then spoke in a carefully casual tone. "Well, it sounds like a joke, but I'm looking for love." He watched Mallory's eyes go wide for a moment before she hid her gleeful reaction. "I've kind of got money burning a hole in my pocket from my great-aunt's inheritance, so I figure it's finally time to settle down." *Bingo.* At the mention of money and marriage, the woman nearly fell off her stool.

"Well, I think that's just *wonderful*," crowed Mallory, flipping her hair and scooting even closer to him.

Each lie came easier to him. Mallory was practically eating out of the palm of his hand. Within the next hour, he managed to make a mysterious reference to his desire to marry quickly, and he even managed to drop a hint that he thought "weddings were too much fuss, and a quick ceremony at the courthouse was much better."

The only setback came when Mallory asked him where Ellie had been taking him lately. Foolishly, Calvin answered with the truth. "Restaurants for lunch, the park, that sort of thing. Tomorrow she's showing me a waterfall."

"The falls? I *love* the falls," cried Mallory dramatically. "Oh my gosh, I've just had the most fantastic idea! Why don't I go with the two of you? Ellie and I are old friends. It would be *such* fun."

"Well…" said Calvin. He thought he remembered Ellie saying something different about their possible "friendship."

"You should come along," he said reluctantly. He didn't really want her to go, but he couldn't think of a polite way to say no.

"Wonderful!" she cried. "I'll call Ellie in the morning and get a ride with her." She shifted in the stool, managing to pull her dress down even further in the process. "Now, tell me, what's it like being a stockbroker? It sounds *so* exciting."

Calvin suppressed a sigh. It was going to be a long night.

***

Ellie was puttering around her kitchen making a cup of coffee when her phone rang the next morning.

"Hello?" she answered. She hadn't recognized the number on the caller ID. Maybe it was the movers at Calvin's house, but she had given them really clear directions the day before.

"Hi, Ellie, honey?"

"Yes?"

"It's Mallory Evans! I was with Calvin last night, and he mentioned you guys were going to the falls today. I'd *love* to tag along with you when you drive up. I'd have called last night, but it was too late when Calvin mentioned it to me."

Ellie's stomach clenched at the other woman's syrupy-sweet voice. *She had been with Calvin? As in, stayed the night with him?* She didn't want to think it was true, but… boys had always liked Mallory better than they'd liked Ellie.

"Ellie? Are you there?"

"Yeah, sorry. Yeah. Sure you can ride with me. Not a problem. Just be at my place at two."

After a few more polite words, Ellie ended the call and sat down numbly at her kitchen table. She felt betrayed. Why had Calvin invited someone else on their adventure? It made sense now that he hadn't kissed her yesterday, even though she'd practically given him an open invitation. *God.* She'd been falling for him more every day, and he'd been dating Mallory this whole time.

By the time the other woman was in her car, Ellie had developed a pounding migraine. Mallory's incessant chatter wasn't improving the headache or her mood, either. The woman would *not* shut up about Calvin.

"He's *so* sophisticated," she yammered. "And rich. I can totally tell. But it's so weird—he told me he wants a courthouse wedding, even though he's obviously so stylish."

Ellie's head snapped to the side so she could stare at Mallory. "You guys have talked about *marriage?*" She tried to sound casual, but some of her intensity came through in her tone.

"Oh, sure," said the dark-haired woman. "He told me he's in a hurry to settle down. And I can tell you—I'm planning on being the one he settles down with. I would make the *perfect* society wife for him in New York."

Tight pain gripped Ellie's throat at her old classmate's words. She suddenly remembered what he'd told her about wanting to give the women of

Carterville a chance. Clearly, he was giving Mallory more than a chance. Ellie regretted ever introducing them.

Things didn't get any better when they met up with Calvin. He was outside and leaning against his rental car at the trailhead by the time they pulled up, and even as Ellie put the parking brake on Mallory was jumping out and running to kiss him on the cheek.

"Hey, Ellie," Calvin said, with Mallory clinging to his arm, when she got out of the car.

"Hi," she said. "Everything working out okay with the movers?" She was afraid her voice was glacial, but the other option was crying. She would just have to be icy cold to Calvin and cry when she got home that night.

"Sure," said Calvin. "They seem to know what they're doing. Showed up bright and early and got down to business. Professional and friendly."

"Good," said Ellie, with a faint quiver to her voice. She moved away and let Calvin stay with Mallory.

As they headed down the trail, Ellie led the way, moving quickly. She just wanted to get away from the happy couple behind her. Mallory still hung on Calvin's arm, and she could hear the woman giggling as they walked.

The idiot woman was wearing heels, as opposed to Ellie's sensible sneakers, so it was easy to outpace her.

For a blissful twenty minutes, Ellie managed to stay far enough ahead that she could pretend she was alone. The path was familiar, and the cool woods were soothing—until a loud squeal echoed from back along the trail.

She jogged back around the corner to see Mallory sitting in the dirt, whimpering, and Calvin sitting next to her feeling the joint of her ankle. "It feels fine," he said. "Just a sprain if anything. But I think you just rolled it."

"Ugh!" whined Mallory. "I hate it out here!"

Ellie suppressed a bitter snicker as she walked up alongside the pair.

"I thought you said you loved the falls," Calvin was saying.

"Oh," said the other woman stupidly. "Uh, I do. Just not the walk to them." She grinned winningly up at him, but somehow Ellie thought he wasn't buying it.

"Owww," whined Mallory. "Calvin, baby, I don't know if I can finish the hike. I think we should just go back to the car."

Ellie expected him to give in right away, but the man looked hesitant. He looked longingly down the trail and then back at his date. "I really want to see the falls," he said. "And Ellie drove out here just to show me."

Mallory became immediately petulant. "Really?" she asked, pouting.

"We're so close," Ellie chimed in, unable to resist causing trouble. "It's just a few corners up the trail."

Mallory's lower lip quivered under a heavy coat of lip gloss, but Calvin wasn't swayed. "You'll be fine here," he said, patting the woman on the arm.

Victory! With a polite smile, Ellie took off back down the trail. Maybe Calvin saw right through Mallory after all. She was so nasty, and Calvin seemed so wonderful. Still, she couldn't forgive him enough to talk openly like they had been.

The pain of his betrayal hit her all over again, and she took off at a fast pace again, leaving Calvin a few steps behind. Their feet thumped against the dirt trail, but otherwise the silence of the woods was unbroken. Ellie took deep breaths, trying to feel serene, and it almost worked. She really did love it out here.

Calvin was quiet, but he stared around in all directions, and Ellie wondered what he was thinking about.

"It's just down the hill," she said, gesturing at the corner of the trail. He nodded, and she took a breath and said what she really wanted as they walked forward. "So, you and Mallory, huh?"

"No," said Calvin, sounding startled. "Uh... Well, yes, but..." Ellie stared at him in disbelief, and he just looked defeated. "I guess." They picked their way down the hill together, and he continued, "Thanks for bringing me out here. I'm sorry I didn't ask about inviting Mallory—she kind of invited herself."

Against her better judgment, Ellie softened. "It's fine. I just—I guess I was just hoping—"

***

"Hoping what?" Out of the corner of his eye, Calvin could see that they had reached the waterfall, but he was only looking at Ellie.

He watched her take a deep breath before speaking. "I guess I was hoping that you would be interested in me. I don't mean to be a bad sport about it, though."

Her voice was tiny and pitiful and defeated sounding. "Oh, Ellie…" he said, feeling helpless and startled. He took a step closer to her. *I was hoping that too,* he wanted to say—but he couldn't.

"Sorry," she said very softly. She finally looked up at him again and he could see tears shimmering in her eyes. That was the final straw.

Without stopping to overthink things, Calvin lifted her chin and met her lips with his own.

For a moment, Ellie stood frozen, not resisting but not doing anything else, but then she relaxed into his embrace. Her lips softened and her arms went around his neck as he deepened the kiss. The world around him was entirely lost except for her soft skin, the sweet smell of her perfume, and the gentle caress of her lips against his.

He felt Ellie sigh a little, and he responded by pulling her closer, but suddenly she stiffened up.

"What is it?" Calvin asked, breaking the kiss but staying very close.

Ellie pushed back out of his arms. "You're with Mallory," she said uncomfortably.

"But Ellie, listen, I—"

"No." She whirled away and headed back up the path. "There isn't anything left to talk about."

The euphoric feeling of joy faded from Calvin's brain, and he was left standing there hopeless as Ellie jogged away.

He didn't want to be with Mallory in the least, didn't even want to see her again. The woman had been stupid enough to wear heels hiking, and then audacious enough to whine when she hurt her ankle. On top of that, she'd literally thrown herself at him the night before, and he'd barely managed to stave her off with an excuse about not liking "casual sex."

Her sloppy, forced kiss had been nothing like what had just happened with Ellie. Beautiful, kind, wonderful Ellie, who had claimed his heart almost as soon as he arrived in Carterville. Ellie, who he had been falling in love with for weeks. Calvin suddenly made a decision and took off up the trail.

By the time he reached Mallory, she was standing up indignantly with her hands on her hips—with no sign of a hurt ankle. "Calvin, baby, you just *left* me, and Ellie just ran by me and *ignored* me! She is such a cow!"

"This isn't going to work."

The woman gaped at him. "I—Wha—"

"Us. We are not going to work. Come on. I'll take you home." Calvin slowed his pace to make sure she could keep up, but walked forward without looking back. He ignored every single thing that Mallory whined at him, desperate to catch up to Ellie, but by the time they reached the parking area she was long gone.

Mallory climbed in his car and glared sullenly. "Oh my God. I knew it. You and *Ellie*."

Yes, sang Calvin's heart, but he didn't say anything in response.

When he got home, there were still a few men that he didn't know moving chairs into a truck. He waved but didn't bother talking to them. He was in far too much of a pickle to be friendly and social, and they seemed to be managing things just fine. Instead, Calvin jogged upstairs to the guest room and called Ellie's number.

She didn't answer, which didn't surprise him, so he just left a quick message saying that he'd see her the next day and that they'd talk then. If he remembered right, she should be coming in to check on the moving crew—and if she didn't show up at the house maybe he'd find a reason to drop by the store.

With that done, he flopped over on the bed and stared at the wall. The bedside table had the box of diaries, which reminded him painfully of Ellie, and even worse, that opal ring that she'd thought was so pretty. A heartfelt sigh escaped his lungs. *What am I going to do?* He couldn't possibly be with anyone but Ellie. That was clear now. But he only had a month to marry before he lost the inheritance.

There were no easy answers to the dilemma, so Calvin gave up thinking on it and went to find the oldest box of his great-aunt's diaries. He was going to start at the very beginning and read all of them. At least he could find the answer to one question.

Chapter 10

When Ellie opened the door of the house the next morning, she didn't know what she was expecting. Maybe she thought Calvin would grab her and kiss her all over again, or maybe that he would revert to being entirely distant—but instead, when she followed his call of "Upstairs!" she found him sitting at the library amid piles of books, looking wild-eyed and exhausted. He had not shaved yet, but the beginnings of a beard only seemed to make him look more attractive.

"Ellie, you're not going to believe it!" he said enthusiastically.

"Believe what? Have you slept?" Her brow furrowed in concern.

Calvin brushed it off. "I started reading the diaries. I think I know who he is!" Calvin held up one of the old photos they had discovered, and Ellie realized that the old chest was in here too, amid the leather-bound diaries.

"Seriously?" For a moment, she forgot everything but her curiosity.

"Yes! Loretta started keeping a diary when she was like 15—but only a few entries in, she mentions meeting a boy who was visiting from out of town. His

111

name was Edward, *just like the family in the newspaper article.* Edward Talbot. I think that's him." Calvin gestured around, clearly looking for the newspaper clipping, but shrugged when he couldn't find it.

"It was love at first sight—for Great-Aunt Loretta, anyway. But then the Talbots left again after the summer and she was so heartbroken. That's when she switched to writing the diary entries to 'You'—I think 'you' is Edward. The boy she loved!"

"Oh wow," said Ellie, staring at the pile of diaries. "And she kept writing to him for her whole life? What happened?"

"Well, things get happier for a little while, kind of. Her life was pretty tough, but Edward and his family came back visiting two summers in a row. The only problem is that Loretta wasn't allowed to write to him. It sounds like his family didn't approve."

"How sad." She could feel the pain the other woman must have felt, still a teenager but already being told she wasn't good enough.

"Mhm. Listen. 'I don't know how much I can bear being away from you, my love. It seems forever until June, even if it's only two more miserable months. Surely, now that you are of legal age, we can be together.' But that didn't work out. Listen to this one the next summer."

Calvin dug around wildly in the pile for another diary. "Sorry," he added as an aside, seeming sheepish. "I was up all night reading these. I couldn't stop. I hope we don't have anything to work on."

"It's okay," she said, chattering nervously. "They'll pull out the rest of the furniture today, but we just have to stay out of the way. It should be fine to read. They don't need the books." She closed her mouth sheepishly, realizing that she was babbling.

"Aha!" He held up a volume victoriously, seeming not to have heard anything she'd said, and opened to a page marked by a ribbon. "'Oh, dearest, I don't know what madness you've led me into. My head is all awhirl with what we've done. I feel so happy, but also not, all at once. I don't think I could deny you anything—nor you me, at least in that moment this afternoon. But all the same, I know this is wrong. We can't go on like this. Surely now you'll marry me! I don't care what your parents will think. Our love is real.'"

Fascinated, Ellie held out her hand for the diary, and stared down at the angst-filled words on the page. "So they became lovers," she breathed.

"Yes, I think so!" said Calvin, his blue eyes shining in excitement. "She risked her reputation—but I guess he never did marry her. That's as far as I've gotten."

For a moment, they rested there, eyes locked on one another. "Ellie, listen," said Calvin, suddenly sounding very serious. "I'm not with Mallory. I told her I won't be seeing her anymore."

Ellie felt her eyes go wide. She didn't know what to say. Was it possible? Could he really be interested in her instead? The hope that she had kept buried in her chest sprang to the surface. "Are you sure?" she asked softly. "I… I really want to be with you, Calvin. But you haven't seemed interested."

"Ellie, look. I want to be with you. Just you. I was being an idiot."

Her mouth was dry as she responded. "Why now? What changed?"

Calvin stood up and moved before her, and she felt her breathing speed up nervously. "I didn't even like Mallory, honestly. That was only our second date. But, Ellie, yesterday, standing there by the waterfall, it hit me how much I feel for you. And now, reading these"—he gestured at the diaries on the table—"I don't want that to be us. I don't want one of us pining after the other for a lifetime."

"Oh," she said. This close she could see each eyelash that framed his gorgeous, deep blue eyes.

"And that kiss, Ellie… It was mind-blowing." Though Calvin sounded calm, Ellie saw him swallow nervously.

"It was," she breathed. They stood together for a moment, frozen.

Instead of waiting for him to make the move, this time Ellie led. Her lips brushed his cautiously and then caught, deepening into a slow, sweet kiss. Calvin's mouth was gentle but firm, and as the embrace intensified, he slid a hand into her hair and pulled her tighter to him.

"Ellie," he said, breaking away for moment, "I'm so sorry about yesterday. I don't want to lose you."

She had to catch her breath before replying. "You're not seeing Mallory anymore, right?" She still felt vulnerable from yesterday's shock.

"No," he said. "Trust me, please. I'm sorry I didn't mention it to you in the first place."

***

Calvin looked at Ellie's wide vulnerable eyes and her pretty pink cheeks and knew he'd meant what he just said. He wanted this woman to trust him absolutely.

She laid her head on his shoulder and murmured, "Of course I trust you," and a knife of guilt twisted in his stomach. She had no idea that he'd been lying to her—lying to everyone about why he was in Carterville. Calvin looked down at the soft waves of Ellie's hair against his shirt and felt how perfectly she fit into his arms. He didn't want to leave her.

He made a decision. It had seemed hard, but now, looking down at Ellie, it was incredibly easy.

He wasn't going to take the inheritance. It wouldn't be right to take advantage of Ellie and try to rush her into marriage for the sake of money. "Ellie," he said slowly, tipping her face up toward him, and stealing another quick kiss, "I know it's early for this, but I need you to hear something. I—I really care about you. I will do whatever it takes to be with you. I don't know if you feel the same, but—"

Ellie gasped softly, lips parting and eyes lighting up. "Calvin, I…"

"Shh, just listen," he said. He silenced her with another kiss, though this one lasted rather longer than intended. Breathing shakily, he finally broke it and continued. "I have to go back to New York soon. I took a three-month leave of absence, but that's nearly over and if I don't go back I'll lose my job. I don't want to leave you, and I swear we'll make it work somehow, but for a while it's going to be tough." He wasn't quite brave enough to reveal exactly how deeply he felt for her, or explain why he'd come out here in the first place, but he needed Ellie to know that he was really committed.

"Oh." Sadness tinged the corners of her coffee-colored eyes, but then she smiled with forced cheer. "Well, I guess we'd better not waste a moment then." She tugged his face back to level with hers and kissed him again, pausing only to add one thing. "Oh, and of course I feel the same. Why do you think I kept coming back?"

Calvin responded by picking her up and kissing her deeply as he twirled her around in a circle. "That's wonderful news," he said warmly. He kissed her again, tasting her warm lips. "Wonderful. Can I take you to dinner to celebrate?" He grinned wildly at her, looking much younger than he had.

"Well," Ellie said, looking longingly back at the books on the table, "what if you made dinner and we stayed here? We could find out what happened with your great-aunt and Edward."

"Hmmm." Calvin pretended to mull it over, but he thought it was actually a great idea. "Well…" he said teasingly, "I suppose we might be able to do that. On one condition?"

"Yes?" Ellie's eyes lit up as she caught on to his teasing mood.

"We can read the diaries, *if* you sit in my lap and let me steal kisses while we do so." For good measure, he leaned forward and dropped another tiny kiss on the corner of her mouth.

Ellie giggled. "Oh, I think I could manage that."

They spent the afternoon choosing upholstery fabric together, and Calvin felt the warm, blissful feeling of complete happiness overtake him. The work crew she'd hired was still moving things around, so they kept things mellow and almost professional in front of them, but he still spent most of the time holding her soft, small hand and stealing a kiss whenever he could.

When the work day was over, together they made a quick but delicious spaghetti dinner and then settled down with the box of diaries. After Ellie reminded him that the sofa and other downstairs chairs were out being reupholstered, they ended up in the guest bedroom, snuggled into Calvin's bed.

At first, it was hard to focus on the books with Ellie right there next to him in a bed, but Calvin told himself to be patient. There was time to let things develop naturally—and he really did want to find out what had happened with Loretta and Edward. Was he the one who had given his great-aunt her money?

Calvin read page after page out loud, with Ellie's head pillowed on his shoulder. They relived his great-aunt's pain as a young woman, when she gave up her virtue as part of a gamble that didn't pay off. Edward left after the summer, still insistent that his family wouldn't approve of their relationship and unwilling to marry Loretta, even though he claimed to love her. The pages that followed were angry and sometimes tear-stained, as young Loretta wrote letter after angry letter that she couldn't even send.

Then he turned the page and felt a bombshell hit. "I suppose I should have foreseen this," he read. "We knew the risk we took. But Edward, for this to happen now, and me with no way to write you… I have not had my monthly since before you left, and I can feel a slight swell to my belly now. There is no denying it, and I think I will be delivered of him or her before you ever return. Oh, how could you leave me to this on my own? Thank God, it is only Maude that I have to tell—if Mama and Daddy were still here I do believe they'd kill me."

"Oh my God," said Ellie. "She was pregnant."

Calvin stared at the page for a long, quiet minute. "Not much she could have done about it in those days," he said. "Not in a small town like this. She couldn't raise a child alone without becoming a pariah."

"And no way to tell Edward…" Calvin squeezed Ellie closer and dropped a kiss on her forehead at the pain in her voice. "I wonder what she did," Ellie continued.

"Well, let's find out," Calvin answered, turning the page—but he had a growing suspicion in the back of his head that he didn't want to put words to yet.

They read on, discovering that Loretta had written to her sister Maude—Calvin's grandma—in California, where she was living with her husband, John.

Whatever the exact communication had been didn't make it into the diary, but Loretta was first distraught over her sister's harsh words and then incredibly grateful for her kindness.

Calvin's eyes flew over the page. "Though I begged her not to, Maude has told John, and perhaps it was for the best because they have come up with a solution. They shall drive up to get me this weekend, and I will come stay with them until the baby is born. Maude has put word out that she is expecting, and when the child is born I shall give it up to her. I wanted to call him Edward, for you, but Maude insists that if she is to raise the child, it shall be called Philip for our father or—" Calvin's voice broke. "Or Ann, for our dear, departed mother."

Ellie turned to look at Calvin, who was staring at the page in disbelief. "So your grandmother raised Loretta's child alongside her own? Was…" She trailed off, clearly not knowing how to continue, and Calvin took a deep, steadying breath.

"My mother's name was Ann," he said, hoarse with emotion. "The baby was my mother."

***

Ellie tentatively reached over and grasped his hand. "Are you okay?" she asked uncertainly. This was all too new for her to be certain where she stood with Calvin, or how to comfort him when he was upset.

"Yeah, I'm fine. Thanks," he said, squeezing her hand. "Guess it's just kind of a shock."

"Do you want to keep reading? We could take a break."

"Yeah, actually," Calvin said. "I'd like to hear how it all played out. Would you mind taking over, though? My voice is tired."

Ellie nodded and took the book from his strong hands. She started where he left off, and enjoyed the safe warm feeling of his body next to hers and the suspense of the pages as she read the slanted cursive handwriting.

At some point, as she relayed the boredom of young Loretta's days at a house she hadn't been allowed to leave for fear of a ruined reputation, the pain of Ann's birth, and then the sad and lonely days of her return to Carterville, Calvin's head settled on her shoulder and his breathing deepened. She looked over and saw him peacefully sleeping, face relaxed. It was adorable.

She thought about sitting the book down, slipping out of the house, and leaving, but the story was too enticing and she didn't want to leave Calvin.

Instead, she read on late into the night, discovering how Loretta had at long last seen Edward again the following summer, and told him of their child, and how they had cried together when he told her that it was for the best because he was engaged to a girl his parents approved of. Ellie found tears in her own eyes when she read about the touching scene. She wanted to share this all with Calvin, but he was sound asleep and she couldn't stand to wake him.

Ellie read and read and read, voraciously turning page after page and immersing herself in the life of a woman she'd never met. She read how Edward had pleaded with Loretta until she'd agreed to take his money and visits whenever he could get away from his new wife. She read how when his parents had died in a train crash, he had given his mistress a piece of his inheritance: their vacation home and the very house that Loretta had then left to Calvin.

She read Loretta's shaky hand explaining that Maude had allowed only a few visits between her and Ann, and how those visits wouldn't be happening anymore so they didn't confuse the little girl. Loretta agreed that it was for the best, but the poor, lonely woman was heartbroken, all alone in her giant house waiting for less and less frequent visits from her married lover. Ellie cried again when she read it.

Finally, she turned a page and a small photograph fell out onto her lap—a wide-eyed baby boy. *Maude has written me that Ann and her husband have been delivered of a healthy baby boy. They've called him Calvin, and I think it a fine name. Oh, Edward, if only you were here to see this picture and to admire his fine head of curly hair, just like your own.*

Even if I have not seen you in more than two years, here is a picture of our very own grandbaby and I know you would cherish him as much as I do. I only wish that I could see him and dote on him as Maude can. Even though I've never held him in my hands, I love him so terribly much that it hurts. My Ann has certainly done well by herself.

Without thought, Ellie shook Calvin awake.

"What?" he asked blearily, sitting up and looking around in confusion. "Ellie, have you been crying? What's wrong?"

"Oh, Calvin," Ellie said, close to tears, "your great-aunt loved you so much."

Maybe he was still half asleep, because Calvin didn't grab the diary that she held out to him. Instead, he rolled over and pulled Ellie to him groggily. "Don't cry about it," he said sleepily. "I love you so much, too, you know. You're so sensitive and sweet."

Ellie held her breath, waiting for him to take back his profession of love or realize that he was talking without being all the way awake, but instead he just blinked at the light and pulled her even closer. "Calvin…" said Ellie, breathless as he nuzzled at her neck.

"D'you want me to stop? I will if you say so," he murmured, dropping a line of kisses down the soft skin to her collarbone.

Ellie sighed at the warmth of his caress and tried to think. "No," she said, "you don't need to stop just yet."

Calvin leaned over her and she gave into what she wanted and kissed him thoroughly. "On second thought," she added a few moments afterward, "you don't need to stop until you want to."

And so he didn't stop, at least until much later.

***

In the morning, Calvin woke up when Ellie slid out of his arms and tiptoed into the bathroom. He smiled appreciatively at her mussed hair and attempt at being courteous, and then caught sight of the leather notebook that she had sat on the bedside table.

That was right—Ellie had wanted him to read something the night before. He stretched and grabbed the notebook, flipping it open to the marked entry.

He read the kind, loving words, and then read them again, feeling the slight indents in the paper with his fingers, trying to feel the connection to a woman he'd never known. A shadow reappeared in the doorway, and he looked up to see Ellie.

"Thank you for making sure I read this," he said seriously, smiling a little bit at her sleep-puffed eyes.

"Oh, sure," she answered, fidgeting at the edge of his shirt, which she'd thrown on. The light blue fabric set off her tanned legs perfectly. "I wasn't sure you were going to remember me telling you that. Or anything else we might have talked about last night…"

Calvin grinned, suddenly understanding why she seemed so awkward. "Oh yes," he said. "I remember it all quite clearly."

"Oh," said Ellie, looking shy.

"I meant what I said," he said slowly, watching her carefully to see if her reaction was positive or negative. She turned a brighter shade of red, but he thought he saw a smile curve the edges of her lips as she looked down at her feet.

"Oh," she said again.

"No pressure, though," he added. "I know it's early days." She smiled quite happily at him and he tried not to over-evaluate it. "So what did I miss out on during my nap last night? Did you solve our mystery?"

"Oh! Oh my gosh, I almost forgot." Ellie nearly bounced over to him. "I know where she got the house! It's pretty dramatic, actually."

"Well, enlighten me while I make you breakfast then," he said cheerfully.

In the kitchen, Calvin sizzled a quick scramble of eggs and peppers while Ellie explained how he'd come to own the house they stood in. He listened in astonishment to the whole story: house from Loretta's lover, who he suddenly realized was his grandfather, and guilt payments from the same man instead of visits. On the bright side, Loretta—who he couldn't quite decide whether to call Grandma or Great-Aunt—had apparently become somewhat of an investment maven with tips from Edward. It was maybe the only bright point in a lonely life, but Calvin was overjoyed to hear that his gift with money management might be a hereditary link to his grandmother.

Everything with Ellie just seemed to come so naturally. After she finished explaining everything that the diaries had contained, they ate their breakfast together while holding hands across the table. They cleaned up the dishes together like they'd been doing it for years, and with no hidden tension between them, the day's work on the house flew by.

Before he knew it, two weeks had passed with her at his house almost every night—except for two, which he'd spent with Ellie in her own cute little house. During the day, they had to reluctantly separate so Ellie could go to the shop and he could put the finishing touches on the house, but each evening found them back in one another's arms. The craziest thing was that even with all that, Calvin couldn't get enough of Ellie—her sweet smile, her cheerful laugh, the tenderness and sensitivity that she brought to his life. Sure, she hadn't said that she loved him back, but Calvin was hopeful that it would come in time.

It was a wonderful contrast to when he had first come to Carterville. Instead of spending all day worrying about will provisions and where Loretta Meyer had gotten her money, Calvin was really *living*. In fact, other than continuing to slowly read the diaries, he hadn't even thought about the other things, like the will deadline or when he needed to return to work.

One afternoon, his cellphone rang with a call from Walter Greenfeld's office, but Calvin didn't even have to think before he rejected it. He had no regrets with choosing Ellie over the inheritance. She made him happier than money ever could, and he wasn't going to lie to her and rush her into marriage just so he could get money.

But there was just one problem, which made him sigh when he remembered it. As much as he wanted to stay here in their little bubble of happiness, he had to go back to New York. He had to quit his job, find a sublease for his apartment, and work out a way to move across the country without going bankrupt.

It wasn't going to be easy, and it was going to take time. Weeks, or maybe even months. Later that day, he tried to explain exactly why it bothered him as he and Ellie looked at dishwashers in her store.

"I feel like I've barely begun to have something real and stable and wonderful in my life—my relationship with you—and now I'll be losing it again. I'm afraid it will be like things never happened. I know it won't be forever, but I don't want to revert to that guy who was so rude to you when we first met."

Ellie kissed his cheek soothingly. "Calvin, honey, of course you won't revert. I really know you, in here," she said, putting her hand over his heart. "You're a good person, and I know we're meant to be."

"Meant to be?" Calvin's voice grew soft with wonder. Though Ellie never protested or pulled away when he told her he loved her, neither had she returned the sentiment, and somewhere deep inside he longed for the affirmation.

"Yes, meant to be," she said with a grin lighting up her heart-shaped face. Her brown eyes twinkled up at him in a charming way, and he kissed her for a moment. "What did you think true love meant?" Ellie asked once her lips were free.

"Are you saying that—" He found he couldn't complete the question.

"Yes," said Ellie happily. "Yes. I'm saying that I love you. I'm sorry that it's taken so long for me to say it, but oh, do I mean it. I guess I was just afraid you would change your mind about caring for me."

"Never," he said simply. He felt lightheaded with the revelation. "Never. In fact…"

"What?"

"Ellie, we need to go back to the house."

"Why?" She blinked up at him in obvious confusion. "We haven't chosen a dishwasher yet."

"It can wait," Calvin said. "This is urgent."

***

As he drove her back up to the now-familiar mansion, Ellie tried to figure out what Calvin was up to. He seemed to be incredibly fired up about something, anxiously tapping at the steering wheel as he drove, and she smiled fondly at this little quirk.

When they stepped inside, she grinned happily at the evidence of all the hard work they'd been doing—the freshly painted walls and carefully coordinated furniture looked lovely against the fluffy green carpets. "Calvin, *what* are we doing?" she laughed. "We were just here an hour ago."

"Stay right here," he said mysteriously, and jogged up the stairs.

Ellie waited impatiently, listening to the sounds of the man she loved thumping up the stairs and down the hall. A happy flush ran over her cheeks when she remembered his look of stupefied joy back in the shop. She'd been wanting to tell him that she loved him for days, and it felt wonderful to finally have their shared emotion out in the open. *But what was he up to?* She bounced on the balls of her feet as she waited for him to return.

At last, Calvin jogged back down the stairs. He looked shy, which was odd. Ellie smiled happily at the sight of his handsome face. "Well?" she asked. "Are you willing to let me in on the big secret then?"

He took one knee in front of her, and all thoughts of joking suddenly fled her stupefied mind.

"Elizabeth Parker," he said carefully, looking nervous. "I was going to save this for my last day, but, well…" He grinned sheepishly. "The time just seemed right, I guess. You have made me a happier, kinder, overall better person. You've changed my life in so many wonderful ways, and I can't even imagine living without you. I don't want us to be like Loretta and Edward. I want you to know I will be coming back to you. We don't need to rush into anything, because I know I'm moving awfully fast. But I wanted to have this promise between us when I go." His blue eyes shone seriously up at her, and he took one of her limp hands into his own.

"Ellie," he asked carefully, "will you marry me?"

"Yes," she blurted.

"I only have this ring," Calvin was saying as he opened his hand to reveal a small opal ring, "but I saw that you liked it back when we were packing, and I saved it for you. We could always—" He stopped blabbering, an open-mouthed smile spreading across his face. "Yes? Did you say yes?"

"Yes!" said Ellie again. "Yes, yes, yes!" Instead of waiting for Calvin to get up, she threw herself down to his height and knocked him to the floor. "Oh, Calvin," she said as she kissed all over his face, "how could you think I'd say anything but yes?"

"I don't know," he said, wrapping his arms around her and squeezing tight. "Ellie, I love you. I love you so much. I think I've loved you since the day you told me off."

"I think I've loved you from the moment you walked into my store looking so handsome," she confessed. "And I love the ring! It's perfect as is." Belatedly, Calvin slipped it onto her ring finger and they both started laughing. "Well, almost perfect," she amended. "Once we get it sized down a lot."

Ellie kissed him again quite thoroughly. "We could probably do that later, though."

"Mhm?"

"Mhm. For now you should probably just carry me off to bed."

Calvin complied remarkably quickly.

Chapter 11

Ellie felt like she was walking on a cloud as the days flew by. She told Ann first, who grilled her with about a million questions on whether or not Calvin was suitable before finally giving her begrudging approval, and then she told her mother, who nearly fainted from excitement.

"Oh, Ellie, honey!" the older woman had cried out, fanning herself. "I had almost given up on grandbabies. Oh, I wish your daddy could be here to see this."

The two women shared a teary embrace, and finally her mom pulled back with a faux serious tone. "But, young lady, if I don't meet him immediately, there will be trouble."

Ellie had laughed but complied, and even that had gone brilliantly. Calvin had just about charmed her mother's socks off, and as Ellie watched her laughing more than she had since her husband's death, she fell in love with Calvin even more.

But for all the highs, there were also lows. She didn't spend every moment with her new fiancé, and sometimes when she was working alone in the shop, a dark gloomy mood would hit her.

One evening, as she was sitting in her office balancing the budget, those thoughts just wouldn't go away.

"Ellie, focus," she whispered to herself, resting her head in her hands. The cold metal of her ring, now appropriately sized, caught her attention and she smiled down at it for a moment.

But the smile faded quickly. She picked up her phone and dialed Calvin's number, but closed it before hitting the call button. He was off in Portland, picking out a few antique art pieces for the house. She didn't want to make him sad by sharing her worries, especially when she'd chosen to stay behind. Next, Ellie dialed Ann's number. She let this one ring through, but it only reached a voicemail message.

With a sigh, she ended the call. *I'm not going to get any work done if I can't quit moping around,* she thought.

A spark of inspiration struck, and Ellie reached for a notepad. Calvin was always making lists when he had a problem, so maybe doing that would help her.

Things That are Upsetting Ellie, she titled it.

- Calvin leaving.
- Calvin meeting other women in New York.
- Calvin forgetting me.
- Me dying alone and forgotten like Loretta Meyer.

With a loud sigh, Ellie crumpled up the list and threw it across the room. "What a depressing list," she grumbled aloud. "Calvin would never leave you." *Except that he had to, and it could take months for him to come back. He could be gone longer than they had even been together.*

Finally, Ellie gave up on the bills entirely and went home to her house. She had still slowly been reading through the last of Loretta's diaries, glad to glean any understanding of Calvin's family. The story of the woman's life was incredibly fascinating—Ellie had a half-baked idea to turn the diaries into a published book somehow.

She sat down with a diary, meaning to forget her worries, but a few pages in something caught her eye. *"I wonder what sort of man Calvin has grown into. My grandson, though the word seems odd to write, when I have never really had a child or a husband. With Maude and my sweet Ann both gone, I have no way of knowing what kind of life he lives. I wish I could teach him what I learned from you, my love—that young men are often so much in a hurry to do the right and responsible thing that they break the hearts of the women who love them. If I were in his life, I should teach him that even a girl of meager birth and background from a place as small as Carterville could be worth his time. I would show him that perhaps it is better to follow your heart in marriage instead of waiting for the right time."*

Ellie thought about things for a moment, staring at the wise words of her fiancé's grandmother. Surely this must be a reflection of what Calvin had said Loretta's last wishes were—that he give the girls of Carterville a chance. She smiled to herself. It was certainly lucky for her that he had listened. But still, one line jumped out at her in particular.

A resolution formed in her mind. Calvin was going to return from Portland tomorrow morning, and leave for New York in three days. There was very little time left. So in the morning, she was going to take matters into her own hands.

Decisively, Ellie stood up and went to her closet. She needed to pick an outfit for her wedding.

***

When Calvin pulled into his driveway the next morning, he was delighted to see Ellie sitting by the front door of his house.

"You are just what I wanted to see after a long boring drive," he exclaimed as he got out of the car. She walked over to him with a big smile, and he tugged her into his arms for a proper greeting. "You look beautiful," he added, noting her outfit. She wore a pretty white sundress and wedge heels, and she even had makeup on. "Did we have plans for lunch?"

"Um, kind of," said Ellie. She seemed nervous for some reason, twisting at her engagement ring, but

Calvin wrote it off as his imagination. "We can talk about it after we unload the car."

"Sure," Calvin said easily. "Wait till you see the paintings I picked. There's one I think you'll especially love."

"Cool," said Ellie brightly, but something about it seemed forced. A sense of foreboding twisted in his gut. Had she changed her mind about marrying him? But still, she didn't seem upset, just nervous, and she oohed and aahed appropriately as they moved the artwork into the house.

"Okay," he said once everything was unpacked. "Tell me what's wrong."

Ellie bit her lip. "Nothing's wrong, exactly. I just wanted to talk to you about something."

"So talk, sweetheart," he said gently. "Tell me what's on your mind."

He watched his fiancée take a deep breath. "Okay," she said. "We should sit down."

He led the way to the new brown suede couch and waited patiently. Ellie was staring at her hands and twisting her ring again. "So," she said, "I was thinking about something your great-aunt—er, your grandma—said in her diary."

"Yeah?"

She nodded, visibly swallowing. "She said that a lesson she learned from her own experience was that instead of waiting for the right time and being responsible, sometimes young men should be made to marry quickly and follow their hearts."

Calvin blinked in confusion. "Ellie, honey, I am following my heart. That's why I proposed to you."

"I know," she said anxiously. "But Calvin, I was thinking about it, and I don't want to wait. I don't want to be left behind for months while you try to get your affairs in order. So… So I called the courthouse, and it turns out we could get a marriage license today if we pay the waiver fee to speed the process up. And the judge is available to perform marriages until 5:30 p.m."

He stared in shock. "You want to get married today?"

Ellie nodded quickly. "Yes. I really do. We could ask my mom and Ann as witnesses, and I know your dad isn't close enough to make it, but maybe we could bring him in via webcam. Or if you wanted, we could have the whole fancy ceremony later on once things have settled. And when you go to New York, I'll come too. As your wife."

"You'd come with?" His heart leapt at the thought. "But what about the shop, Ellie?"

She brushed the thought off impatiently with a flick of her hand. "I don't care. I'll close it for a while. It's my own business—I can close it if I want. I can stand the losses if I get to be with you."

Processing everything she'd just said, Calvin nodded slowly. "Married today. Hm... Okay."

"Okay?" squeaked Ellie.

"Yes! Let's do it. Call your mom and Ann."

"Okay!" said Ellie, nearly bouncing up and down on the couch. "I'll call them. You should put on something more suitable." She winked.

"Oh!" Calvin pretended to slap his forehead. "That explains the dress."

Only a few hours later, they took Calvin's rental car into town. Ann and Ellie's mother were meeting them at the courthouse, and afterward they were all going to go out for lunch together. Calvin had declined to bother his father about the whole thing, opting for the possibility of having a fancy wedding later once things were settled.

"I can't believe we're doing this today," Ellie said from the passenger seat, grinning happily at him. Calvin smiled back and grabbed her hand with a squeeze. He couldn't believe it either. His honest expectation had been that Ellie would want to wait months, or even a year—not two weeks.

A nasty voice in the back of his head whispered, *"You're getting married in time to claim the inheritance."* He tried to ignore the thought. Maybe he would tell Ellie about the whole situation and claim the money—or maybe he would just not notify Mr. Greenfeld and let it revert to a charity fund. Either way, he wasn't going to let it cheapen his wedding day with the woman he loved.

"Oh," said Ellie, interrupting his thoughts. "I almost forgot. Mom insisted on reserving us a room at the hotel. I hope you don't mind."

Calvin pulled his head back to the present. "That sounds wonderful, love. As long as I get to marry you."

In only a matter of minutes, he found himself standing before a bored-looking clerk, clutching Ellie's hand. His hands were sweating—or maybe hers were, or maybe both. *No time to back out now,* he thought, but then he realized that he didn't *want* to back out. He really wanted to spend the rest of his life with this woman, father children with her, and live in this tiny little town if it made her happy.

He squeezed her hand tighter and focused on the clerk's words. His heart was thumping so loudly that he could barely hear it, and everything passed by in a blur. All he could think was he was going to be *married. Married to Ellie.* Joy swelled within him.

Calvin stared into Ellie's sparkling brown eyes, nodded in the right places, and said "I do" at the right time. Belatedly, she laughed and pulled off her engagement ring and gave it to him to slide back on her slim finger. Finally, they signed the license, grinning wildly, and Ellie's mother and Ann cheered and clapped as he kissed Ellie.

"We did it," he whispered to her. "We did it, *Mrs. Barnard.*" And then he kissed her again.

"I love you," she murmured.

"I love you too."

***

Ellie couldn't stop grinning. She had never been as happy as she was in this moment, holding hands with the man she loved, flanked on both sides by her best friend and her mother. She only wished her father could have been alive to share this moment, but she couldn't help feeling like his spirit was with them. Before the ceremony, her mom had taken her aside for a quiet moment. She'd whispered, "You look beautiful. Wherever your father is, I'm sure he's looking down thinking the same thing." Ellie kept that thought close as she walked to the car with the three people she loved most in the world.

After a brief negotiation, they decided to go to Susie's for lunch.

"I know it isn't fancy," Calvin explained to Ann and Ellie's mother. "But it was where we had our first date—if you could call it a date."

Ann laughed, having already heard the story, but Ellie's mom gave her a questioning look. As Calvin drove, she explained the whole tale. Reliving each minute just made her even happier to be there now as Calvin's bride, and as they pulled into the parking lot she gave his hand an affectionate squeeze.

Her usual order of a turkey club sandwich was delicious as always, and Ellie just basked in the love that surrounded her as she ate. Anticipating what was to come didn't hurt, either. At one point, Calvin stepped out for a moment, and when he came back in, he leaned over and whispered in her ear, "I just called the hotel and asked them to chill some champagne for our room later. I can't wait."

But perhaps the best moment of all came when Mallory walked inside, talking loudly on the phone. She made it almost to their table before she noticed the group. Feeling mischievous, Ellie ignored her old classmate's irritated expression and waved cheerily.

"Mallory, hi!" she said sweetly.

"Ellie. Hi. Calvin. Ann. Mrs. Parker." Mallory forced a smile, turning up lips that were coated in bright red lipstick, but it lacked any real feeling. "What are you four doing today?"

"Oh," said Ellie's mom unexpectedly, "it's a special day for us, actually! Ellie and Calvin here have just been married! We're celebrating." The older woman grinned angelically as Mallory's mouth dropped open. She sputtered something about congratulations before spinning and leaving, at which point Ellie's mother leaned forward with a conspiratorial grin.

"There you go, darling," she murmured. "Consider that a wedding gift. If I remember right, she was quite nasty to you in high school."

Everyone laughed, and Ellie kissed her mom on the cheek. "Thank you, Mama," she said. "You remember right." She and Calvin shared a private smile.

Finally, Ann went home to her family, with a promise to wear an ugly bridesmaid's dress whenever Ellie wanted, and Mrs. Parker kissed bride and groom on the cheek before sending them off to their hotel room.

Calvin carried Ellie over the threshold, closed the door, and carefully locked it. They lost themselves in one another, whispering words of endearment and love over and over again.

The champagne was warm by the time they got to it.

Early the next morning, Ellie slipped quietly out of bed, smiling at the sleeping figure of her new husband. She was by the side table, headed to the bathroom, when she heard a buzzing sound.

Confused, she looked around, trying to identify the noise. A glowing square on the table caught her attention—Calvin's phone. She picked it up, intending to silence it so he could sleep, but the name on the screen caught her eye. "Great-Aunt Loretta's Lawyer," it said.

Anxiously, Ellie looked at Calvin's snoring form and then back at the phone. She really didn't want to wake him, since they'd been up late. But she also didn't want to miss some urgent communication about the property. Before she could decide, the buzzing stopped, making the decision for her.

She was about to sit the phone back down, but it blinked again. *1 New Voicemail.*

With another glance at Calvin, Ellie slid the phone open and pressed play. She just wanted to make sure it wasn't urgent.

"Mr. Barnard, this is Walter Greenfeld. You never returned my previous calls. I just wanted to remind you, the deadline is fast approaching for the inheritance. You did consent to the terms of the will, and I'm afraid if I don't have documentation of your marriage to a woman whose place of legal residence is Carterville, Oregon, the entirety of the $10 million will be turned over to a charity organization. Please do give me a call and let me know either way, as I need to begin filing the correct forms." The dignified voice rattled off a phone number, but Ellie's blood was rushing too loudly for her to hear it.

"What?" Ellie said it out loud, but her voice was so weak as to be inaudible. She hit play again, hoping that she had somehow misheard.

She hadn't.

"I don't understand," said Ellie. She was shaking.

Calvin sat up in the bed, blinking. "Ellie, sweetheart? What is it?"

"I don't *understand*," she said. Her voice wobbled uneasily, and she bit her lip to keep from crying.

"Don't understand what?" Calvin's voice was still hoarse with sleep, but he sounded concerned suddenly.

"I don't understand why you are getting a call from a lawyer, saying that—that—that you have to *marry* someone in order to get *money*!" By the end of the sentence, Ellie's volume had escalated to a near-yell.

"Um…" Calvin sat bolt upright, suddenly looking much more alert. "Ellie, just listen."

"Listen to what? Are you saying… are you saying it's true?" Tears welled up in her eyes, making it hard to see in the dim room.

Silence reigned for a moment, punctuated only by a sniffle.

"Ellie… I haven't been one hundred percent honest with you. My great-aunt—grandmother, whatever she was—put some strictures on the money she left me. She said that I had to marry a woman from Carterville within three months to get it. But I swear to you, Ellie, *swear* on my mother's grave that I wasn't going to do it. I gave up on that when I met you. You're all I want, Ellie…"

"Oh my God," she said bleakly. "She said it right there in her diary. I didn't even know. *God!* You must have thought it was damn convenient when I wanted to get married just in time. Were you ever going to tell me about the money?" Her tears overflowed with the last words.

"No, listen," said Calvin, jumping out of bed and looking panicked. "It wasn't like that. Of course I was going to tell you! We don't even have to take the money. We can talk about that."

A bitter, humorless laugh tore from Ellie's throat. "Take your stupid money," she said. "There isn't anything to talk about. Have your—your $10 million. But you can't have me." Blindly, she stumbled to where her clothes from the day before sat, and started struggling into them.

"What are you saying?" he asked. He sounded frantic now, but Ellie didn't even care. "I thought you were coming to New York with me. That was why we got married right away. I thought we were going to be together forever." She heard footsteps, and then the familiar warmth of his hand landed on her shoulder.

Ellie jerked away. "Don't touch me," she sobbed. "And don't worry. I'll do whatever it takes for you to get your money, but I'm not going with you. I don't ever want to see you again. God, I must have played right into your hands. Stupid small-town girl who actually believed you might love her."

With her sandals finally stuffed on and the crumpled white dress mostly zipped, Ellie stumbled toward the door.

"I do!" Calvin said. "Ellie, I do. Please, you have to trust me."

"No," Ellie said dully. "No. It's too late." With one agonized backward glance, she walked out the door and down the hall, already dialing Ann for a ride.

***

Calvin sat down blankly on the edge of the bed, still warm from Ellie, and stared at his hands. They were shaking. *How could this be happening?* He'd just had everything, right there in his grasp, and now it was all falling apart.

"Ellie," he murmured. "Ellie!" Suddenly realizing he needed to act, he ran to the door and flung it open. "Ellie?" he called down the hallway—but it was already empty.

He called her phone again and again, pacing back and forth, but there was no answer. When he finally had to check out, he tried to leave without thinking how happily they had arrived the night before as husband and wife, but it was no use. Pain knifed at his heart anyway.

Instead of driving to the mansion, he drove to Ellie's and rang the doorbell. Her car was there, so he knew she should be home, but after a few tense minutes the door opened to reveal Ann.

"Calvin," she said quietly. "You need to go. She doesn't want to see you. I think she's made it quite clear."

"But—" said Calvin. Then his shoulders sagged. "Tell her I love her," he said.

When he got back to the house, he saw that he had a voicemail, and for a moment his heart leapt. But it was just from his manager at work, reminding him that he was expected back Monday. Dully, Calvin started packing. The realization dawned on him gradually—Ellie was right. He hadn't done anything to earn her trust. He hadn't been honest. He didn't deserve to be with someone as wonderful and good as she was.

"But I'm not going to give up," he said to his suitcase. His shoulders firmed up at the thought, and Calvin started packing more quickly.

He just needed a plan of action. There was no reason giving up just because Ellie knew the truth. Decisively, Calvin reached for his phone and called Walter Greenfeld back. Although he knew Ellie hadn't meant it, he was going to take her advice. He was going to claim his inheritance and use it to get his life together. With it, he didn't need to worry about his job or moving expenses. He could focus totally on moving to Carterville and winning back the love of his life.

Chapter 12

It only took three weeks for Calvin to make it back to Carterville. He mulled over the irony of the situation during his flight back—only a few short months before, he'd have done anything to avoid this place. But now, he was desperate to get back to his biological grandmother's home and the woman he loved—if she'd have him.

He hadn't heard a peep out of Ellie since the day she'd walked out of their hotel room. Time and again, he'd called her phone. While he had been giving notice to his company and packing up his apartment, he'd also been desperately trying to reach his wife. At least, he thought she was still his wife—no one had notified him if she'd filed for divorce. But she never answered, and never returned the myriad voicemails he left.

Finally, Calvin had decided to change his tactics. When he got off the plane, he wasn't going to drive straight to Ellie's house and throw himself at her feet, as much as he wanted to. He knew that wouldn't win her over. Instead, he had to prove that he actually cared about her and not the money. Calvin knew just how to do that, and now he just had to make it happen.

***

Ellie stood at the back of the store, dusting off the tops of the washers and dryers. She sighed as she worked, and then suddenly spun toward the door at a slight noise.

Nothing. No one was there.

She sighed again, pushing her hair back out of her face. Ever since she'd found out that Calvin was back in town, she'd been jumpy. He had called her constantly for three weeks, so she was certain that the infuriating man would come straight to her door— but he hadn't. In fact, Calvin had been in Carterville for over a week, and Ellie hadn't seen him at all.

Pain twisted in her gut. His absence just proved what she had thought. Calvin Barnard had married her to get access to his great-aunt's money. It had all been a lie. Ellie twisted anxiously at the ring on her finger. She didn't know why she still wore it, or why she hadn't called a lawyer about getting a divorce. But she couldn't quite let go of hope. Something about Calvin's behavior just didn't make sense to her. After all, she had been the one who rushed him to a wedding, not the other way around. Maybe he had really cared for her.

But if he had, where was he?

Ellie blinked back tears and kept dusting.

Moments later, the bell on the front door jingled and she jumped. Setting the duster down, she turned and started walking toward the front. The bell at the register dinged, and she rolled her eyes. "Coming. Just a minute."

But before she even emerged from between the shelves, the door jingled again, and by the time she could see the front, the store was empty. *What?*

Suddenly she noticed a manila folder on the register counter. *Ellie*, it said on the front. Feeling curious, Ellie flipped it open and blinked. The first sheet was a blueprint, but she wasn't sure what for. She flipped to the next page. This one was an artist's sketch of a large, warehouse-style store. On the front of the sketched building hung a sign that said "Parker Home Design."

Ellie gasped. A budget plan followed the sketch, itemizing the costs of shelving, digital register equipment, a fleet of moving trucks, floor layout furniture, and storage. Then there was a printed property listing for an empty lot at the edge of Carterville, and a few sample marketing flyers. Ellie felt herself tearing up at the printouts. Somehow, someone had understood her dream well enough to get it all on paper. Finally, she turned the last page to reveal a handwritten letter.

She sat down unsteadily in her chair, squinting at the small handwriting.

Ellie,

I know you don't want to talk to me. I even understand why. What I did was unforgivable. But what I need you to understand is that it wasn't about the money. It was only about you. You are the only thing that is important to me, and your dreams are my dreams. We could put the money toward your dream store—all of the contracts are waiting for your approval, and I know you would be amazingly successful. Or if you'd rather, we could just go throw it all in the ocean and forget this ever happened. I don't care as long as I get to have you in my life. I don't want to be the Edward to your Loretta. I'd rather be the Mr. Barnard to your Mrs. Barnard. Please, come back to me.

With all my heart,

Your loving husband.

Ellie was just staring at the letter, clutching the folder to her chest, when the door jingled again.

"Calvin?" Somehow, she'd known it was him before she'd even looked up.

"Ellie," he said. He looked nervous, but also incredibly handsome. Butterflies flooded Ellie's stomach at the sight of his familiar blue eyes and messy hair. *God, she had missed him.* "Did you read it?" he asked uncertainly.

She nodded, swallowing back tears. "I did."

"And?"

"And I don't know. Are you trying to buy me? I don't want to be taken advantage of. If we were to—" She choked on the words. "If we were to get a divorce, I wouldn't try to take any of your money."

"Oh, Ellie, no!" Before she could blink the tears out of her eyes, Calvin was around the edge of the counter and at her side. He clutched her hand earnestly in his warm grasp. "I promise I'm not trying to buy you," he said intently. "I just wanted to show you how much I care about you and how little I care about the money. I meant what I said in the letter. Say the word and we'll go withdraw it all in cash and throw it into the ocean, or burn it, or donate it to whomever you please."

Ellie looked up, finally meeting his gaze. "I guess that would be kind of dumb," she said in a wobbly voice. "Although I would probably like to give to a charity or two."

"Does that mean you'll consider it?" Calvin asked, sounding breathless.

As much as she wanted to, Ellie wasn't so sure that she should give in easily. She looked at their hands, which clung tightly to one another, and back into Calvin's concerned blue eyes.

"Yes," she breathed. "Yes, I think so."

"Oh, Ellie, you will?" Calvin pulled her out of the chair and into a tight, tight hug. "I'll never lie to you again," he swore. "Just stay with me and we'll be so happy. We'll make new, happy memories at the house, and raise beautiful babies who look just like you, and Mallory will just about die of jealousy."

A teary laugh escaped from Ellie as she pressed her face into the warm skin of his neck. "I missed you," she said in a heartfelt way.

He squeezed her even tighter. "I missed you too. I love you so much. Every minute I was without you was miserable."

"For me too," she murmured. "Don't leave me again."

"I won't," he said, kissing her forehead. "I promise."

Epilogue

Ellie squeezed her husband's hand lightly as they stood before the gravestone.

"I'm still not sure about talking to her," Calvin said. "She can't really hear me."

"Go on," said Ellie with a gentle smile. "You need the closure. It will be good for you." Her free hand went to the small of her back as she tried to brace the weight of her growing belly.

"You sure you're okay?" Calvin asked, suddenly concerned. "Do you need to sit down? Is the baby kicking?"

She laughed. "Calvin, relax. I can manage just fine. Go on—talk to her."

With one last concerned look, Calvin stepped forward.

"Hi, Loretta," he said, sounding somewhat self-conscious. "Grandma. I don't know if you can hear me right now, but Ellie—my wife—thinks it would be good for me to try this anyway. And since I love her, I do what she wants." He spun around to flash a bright, breathtaking grin at her, and she smiled and made a shooing motion with her hands.

Calvin turned back and continued, more serious. "Anyway, Grandma Loretta, I wanted to come and say thank you. I wish I would have gotten to know you, but I've read your diaries, and I feel like I at least understand you. Sorry if that's weird," he added, "but Ellie doesn't think you'd mind. So I wanted you to know that I am incredibly grateful for the inheritance that you left me. It isn't just the money, although I'll get to that part in a minute. What I'm most grateful for is that you made me come here to this tiny, wonderful town so I could find my roots, and when I did that I met the woman who changed my life. She is beautiful, and kind, and generous—and from Carterville—and I know you would have loved her. I love her so much that I married her, and now we're going to have a baby. That means you and Edward have a great-grandchild, not just a grandchild. I think you would have liked that."

He shifted on his feet before continuing. "Without you, Loretta, I would still be plodding away in my busy city life. But thanks to your will, instead I am here with my wonderful family, and we have a huge, beautiful, successful furniture and interior design business. We are so happy, Grandma Loretta. We fixed up your house—which I think you would like even more now, although it isn't as flowery as before—and we're even working on having your diaries published, that way you're never forgotten. But I promise you, even if that happens, I will never forget you. Even though I only met you once, I owe just about everything to you and your love for me. So… thank you."

Calvin slowly turned back to Ellie, blinking suspiciously bright eyes. "How was I?" he asked gruffly.

Ellie reached out her hand to take his. "Perfect," she said sweetly. "Absolutely perfect."

Together, they turned and walked out of the graveyard and toward their bright, happy future.

What to read next?

If you liked this book, you will also like *The Weekend Girlfriend*. Another interesting book is *Two Reasons to Be Single*.

The Weekend Girlfriend

Jessica has worked hard to be the paralegal that hotshot, sexy attorney Kyle needs. Unfortunately he doesn't see her as just his paralegal but also his own personal assistant. When he blames her for a mix-up in his personal life, Jessica sees no other option but to quit, thinking that her time with him is over. Much to her surprise, Kyle makes a proposition to her that she never thought she would hear coming from his lips. He needs a temporary girlfriend for his sister's wedding and he wants her to be that person. Jessica accepts the challenge and finds herself thrown into his world, learning things about him she never knew. The more time she spends with him outside of work, the more she is drawn to Kyle. As the wedding draws near, she finds herself fighting off some strong feelings for the man. When the wedding weekend is over, will Jessica be able to walk away from Kyle with her heart intact?

Two Reasons to Be Single

Olivia Parker has a job doing what she loves, a wonderful family and plenty of friends, but no luck in the love department. Tired of worrying about it, she decides to swear off love completely and focus on all the good things in her life. Just as she makes her firm resolution, Jake Harper arrives in town and knocks her plans into a tailspin. As the excited single ladies of Morning Glory surround the extremely attractive newcomer, Olivia steers clear of the "casserole brigade," as she calls the women, and tries to keep her distance from Jake. Instead, a variety of situations throw them together and they get to know each other better. They both have reasons for not wanting to get involved in a relationship, but the chemistry between them ignites, even as they desperately attempt to keep it at bay. As things heat up between Olivia and Jake, there is an aura of mystery about him that leaves Olivia certain that he is hiding something. When Jake disappears for a few days without telling Olivia that he is going out of town, she hates the way it makes her feel, and it reminds her of why she was giving up on dating in the first place. As Olivia's feelings for Jake grow, so does the need to find out what exactly brought him to Morning Glory and what he's been hiding.

About Emily Walters

Emily Walters lives in California with her beloved husband, three daughters, and two dogs. She began writing after high school, but it took her ten long years of writing for newspapers and magazines until she realized that fiction is her real passion. Emily likes to create a mental movie in her reader's mind about charismatic characters, their passionate relationships and interesting adventures. When she isn't writing romantic stories, she can be found reading a fiction book, jogging, or traveling with her family. She loves Starbucks, Matt Damon and Argentinian tango.

One Last Thing...

If you believe that *Investment in Love* is worth sharing, would you spend a minute to let your friends know about it?

If this book lets them have a great time, they will be enormously grateful to you – as will I.

Emily

www.EmilyWaltersBooks.com

Printed in Great Britain
by Amazon